"Lily?" It was both question and entreaty, begging her for permission, and she nodded, lips half parted in anticipation.

Primal need filled him. Damir wanted nothing more than to rush, to crush her to him, to explore her mouth, her body, to hear her moan and sigh and call his name, to tumble her onto the ground and cover her with his body. He wanted to tear at their clothes, for there to be no barriers between them. And he could do it, he knew it, sensed it—the air around them danced with the haze of desire; she wanted him as much as he wanted her. But he held himself back.

Slowly, every movement full of intent, he pulled her to him. She was tall, but still a head shorter than him, and he had to dip his head to taste her. It was a light kiss, an exploratory kiss, an anticipatory promise of what could be, and it overwhelmed him like no kiss had for longer than he cared to remember.

Dear Reader,

I wrote this book during what seemed like nonstop rain and flooding, and edited it while in lockdown due to COVID-19. I have never been so grateful to be able to mentally step into another world, drawing on my memories of a recent sun-filled holiday in the beautiful city of Dubrovnik and some of the wonderful places I visited during that time. I can't wait to return there one day soon.

Lily and Damir are both in their own dark places at the beginning of the book. Reeling after her best friend's tragic accident, Lily agrees to manage her grandmother's small B and B on an idyllic island, where she meets Damir, driven, single-minded and determined to get his hands on that very B and B. An accidental meeting on the beach gives him the in he needs, but he doesn't expect to find Lily so very appealing. Soon he has to ask himself what's more important. Fulfilling his father's dreams, or chasing after his own? Meanwhile, Lily is wondering if she's brave enough to step away from the rigid life plan she made as a teenager and risk her heart in the process.

Love,

Jessica

Mediterranean Fling to Wedding Ring

Jessica Gilmore

Recycling programs
for this product may
not exist in your area.

ISBN-13: 978-1-335-55656-1

Mediterranean Fling to Wedding Ring

Copyright © 2020 by Jessica Gilmore

This edition published by arrangement with Harlequin Books S.A.

For questions and comments about the quality of this book,
please contact us at CustomerService@Harlequin.com.

Harlequin Enterprises ULC
22 Adelaide St. West, 40th Floor
Toronto, Ontario M5H 4E3, Canada
www.Harlequin.com

Printed in U.S.A.

A former au pair, bookseller, marketing manager and seafront trader, **Jessica Gilmore** now works for an environmental charity in York, England. Married with one daughter, one fluffy dog and two dog-loathing cats, she spends her time avoiding housework and can usually be found with her nose in a book. Jessica writes emotional romance with a hint of humor, a splash of sunshine and a great deal of delicious food—and equally delicious heroes!

Books by Jessica Gilmore

Harlequin Romance

Fairytale Brides

Honeymooning with Her Brazilian Boss
Cinderella's Secret Royal Fling
Reawakened by His Christmas Kiss
Bound by the Prince's Baby

Wedding Island

Baby Surprise for the Spanish Billionaire

Summer at Villa Rosa

A Proposal from the Crown Prince

Maids Under the Mistletoe

Her New Year Baby Secret

The Sheikh's Pregnant Bride
Summer Romance with the Italian Tycoon

Visit the Author Profile page
at Harlequin.com for more titles.

For Sally. Hopefully by the time this is published we will have danced at your wedding and you'll be planning your Croatian honeymoon. Xxx

Praise for
Jessica Gilmore

"Totally loved every page. I was hooked right into the story, reading every single word. This book has to be my new favorite. Honestly this book is most entertaining."

—*Goodreads* on
Honeymooning with Her Brazilian Boss

CHAPTER ONE

A GOLDEN SLANT of sunshine broke through a chink in the curtains to shine directly onto Lily's closed eyelids. She muttered, moving to escape the brightness, but with that movement came consciousness. She wasn't in her own bed, on her expensive sprung mattress, between her four hundred thread Egyptian cotton sheets, but on an old iron bedstead in a plain white walled room. Despite that she'd slept more deeply than she had for months.

Squinting a little against the sunlight, Lily slipped out of bed and padded across the cold tiled floor to throw open the curtains and to take her first proper look out of the wooden framed window. She inhaled sharply. Sky so blue it defined the colour greeted her, lit by an early morning silvery sun. For the first time in several months the pain inside Lily's chest eased. It felt as if it had done nothing but rain all year in England, and on the few dry days glowering cloud still greyed the sky. This vibrant, warm Croatian beauty was as foreign to her as the language and currency, but so very welcome.

She'd arrived late the evening before, a delayed plane meaning it was already dark by the time she'd cleared passport control, retrieved her bags and stumbled into a waiting taxi. The long day of delays and airports had left her so tired and wrung out she'd barely squinted out of the car window into the dark to try and get any idea of her surroundings. Even the night-time boat ride bringing her to the small island of Lokvar had failed to excite her, it was if she had brought the London gloom with her.

But the beauty of the early morning scene cleared the last remnants of that gloom, instead a hint of anticipation filled her. Reluctantly dragging herself away from the window, Lily darted into the small adjoining bathroom, jumping into the shower to clean the travel grime and sleep from her body, slipping into her comfiest jeans and a

T-shirt and bundling her still-wet hair into a loose bun. Less than ten minutes later she was ready to go, running down the winding staircase that led to the main hallway of the large, empty villa.

Empty now, but in just a few weeks this villa would be filled to capacity with holidaymakers all relying on her and her team to ensure their stay ran smoothly. She looked over at the reception desk and her stomach clenched. It seemed impossible that just a week ago she had been Lily Woodhouse, lawyer, London dweller, city worker who routinely worked sixty-hour weeks and rarely saw daylight. What did she know about running a hotel, let alone a hotel in a country where she didn't speak the language, on an island with no cars and just three boats daily into Dubrovnik?

Fighting back the panic, Lily did her best to regulate her breathing, concentrating on inhaling and exhaling until the panic began to fade away, answering each of her panicked mind's questions as calmly as she could. She wouldn't be alone here, experienced help was on its way, and she still had time to find her feet before the tourist season really swung into action and the island welcomed the hordes of visitors who visited every summer. Today she was allowed to take time out and settle in. Today she was going to explore.

She'd bolted the villa's front door the night before, even though common sense had told her that on an island of barely three hundred residents and no way in or out other than by boat, she was safer with an unlocked door than she was behind the padlocks of her London apartment, but old habits died hard and over the last few months Lily had learned all about regret. Slipping her feet into her discarded trainers and grabbing her bag, she unlocked the door and wrenched it open before stepping outside, fumbling for her sunglasses as her eyes adjusted to the light.

The view from the window was nothing compared to the real thing. It might be early but the sun was already warm and she felt its welcome heat permeating through to her tired, tired bones whilst the vibrant colours—green, blue, turquoise—warmed her soul.

The villa faced onto a wide shallow cove,

the beach sandy, unusual on this famously rocky coastline. The only building on this side of the island, it ran as a B&B and a beach café through the summer months, a reasonable part of its income derived by renting beach chairs, sunbeds and umbrellas to the day trippers escaping the heat and crowds of Dubrovnik. Lily had never visited Lokvar before, she hadn't even been to Croatia, but she'd seen so many pictures of the villa and Fire Cove, she felt like she'd come home.

Her stepfather, Josip, had described his boyhood home to her many times, and every autumn, after the season ended, his mother, Lily's *baka*, spent several months with them, full of stories about the season just gone, her guests and staff and her friends and neighbours who lived on Lokvar year-round. Josip would sometimes join in, but too often he would leave the room, jaw tight and eyes shuttered. He'd left Dubrovnik at the end of the Balkan conflict, never to return. Lily had never asked why, not knowing how to frame the question, but as she breathed in the fresh sea air and her eyes drank in the glorious scenery she knew his reasons must be deep and dark to prevent him from returning to such beauty.

As if on cue her phone buzzed and Josip's name filled the screen. She fumbled to answer the call, walking down the beach to watch the soft waves roll in as she did so. 'Hi. What time is it there?'

'Six, but your mother couldn't sleep until she knew you were okay.' Lily could hear the smile in his voice as her mother called out something she couldn't quite hear. Josip had lived in the UK for nearly thirty years now, his accent softened but still clear, and her heart filled with love for the man who had brought stability and peace to her turbulent childhood.

'I texted when I arrived last night,' she protested.

'I know that and you know that, but you know how your mother is.' Lily did know, just as she knew her mother would have liked to have accompanied Lily over to Lokvar and helped her ready the B&B for the season ahead, always trying to make up for the chaotic first decade of Lily's life. But she didn't like to travel anywhere without Josip, and he couldn't or wouldn't return to Croatia. Lily prided herself on her independence, but she had to admit that part of her would have liked her mother and her stepfather here as she negotiated her way through the start of her summer.

'Well, tell her I'm fine, at least I will be when I have found some coffee and breakfast.'

'And make sure you get your first grocery order in. Everything is delivered from the mainland, so you need to plan in advance. Ana will be with you tomorrow, she has worked at the villa for years, she will be able to help you with anything you need.'

'I know. I am so glad she has agreed to come early and help me prepare.' The truth was that Ana, Josip's cousin, could quite easily have run the villa without any of Lily's input, having assisted her aunt for the last decade or so. But Lily had needed a change of scene and direction and so when Marija, her step-grandmother, had announced her intention of taking a summer off while she visited cousins in America and New Zealand, Josip had persuaded

Lily that the only way his mother would be able to fully enjoy her time away would be if she knew that Lily was keeping an eye on her home.

'She's not getting any younger and I think she needs to take the time to really rest and relax,' he had told Lily. 'I know she spends a couple of months with us every year, but London in late autumn and early winter is so damp and cold, she doesn't get out much. She deserves the chance to really enjoy her time off.'

There was just enough truth in that statement for Lily to agree without feeling too manipulated. It was becoming clear that running her beloved B&B was starting to take its toll on seventy-year-old Marija, and every November she arrived in London looking a little frailer than the year before.

She had confided in Lily that she had received a very lucrative offer for the villa at the end of the last season, but the buyer wanted the land and the access to the beach, not the graceful old villa that had been in her family for generations. 'I want my Josip to return one day, not sell his birthright out from under him,' she had said with a sigh.

Lily just wished she had actually spent a summer here with Marija, after all she'd been invited often enough. But then there were so many things she wished she'd done differently. Too many to name.

She wrenched her attention back to the here and now as her stepfather spoke. 'So what are your plans for today? After coffee, of course.' The jocularity in Josip's voice didn't hide his worry, and Lily hated that she was responsible for it.

'Explore, start making lists of what we have to do,' she said as carelessly as she could, as if getting a small B&B ready for the start of a busy season was completely part of her skill set. 'Maybe a little sun-bathing while I have time. I know it'll be harder to relax once the tourists arrive.'

'Well, enjoy. And, Lily? Let me know if you need anything at all.'

'I will,' she promised. 'Love to Mum.' Lily swallowed as she disconnected the call, as if by doing so she had disconnected herself from her life. But then her life had already been disconnected three months ago when she'd received the phone call telling her that Izzy, her best friend and flatmate, had been knocked off her bike and was in a coma, and her world and everything she'd thought she knew about who she was and what she wanted had shattered irrevocably.

Inhaling deeply, Lily slipped her phone into her pocket. She was here to make a new start, to try and make some sense of her life. To try and live differently, to *be* different. More spontaneous, impulsive, to actually live her life, not plan her way through it. And she couldn't do that by dwelling on the past. '*Carpe diem*,' she said, her voice wavering as she said the words.

Her old motto, one she and Izzy had adopted at school as they'd competed for the top grades, the top prizes, the university places, had been an only semi-ironic *Veni, Vidi, Vici*. Young, bright and ambitious, they had been so sure that the world was theirs for the taking. And it had been, until a lorry had taken a reckless turn and in one screech of brakes had made a waste of all Izzy's talent and brains, her careful plans, her savings and dreams. So much time spent working and planning, so little time spent actually living. Lily had stood by Izzy's hospital bed and promised her comatose friend that she would do enough living for the both of them. Now she just had to figure out how.

Her new motto felt strange in her mouth. '*Carpe diem*,' she said again. Louder this time. 'Seize the day!' And then again and again until she was yelling it out to sea, hoping that by sending the words out across the waves and into the sea she could somehow make them true. Somehow.

Damir rounded the sandy path leading to Fire Cove and paused. Someone was shouting, calling out as if all the hounds of hell were after them. Adrenaline spiked. Lokvar was one of the safest places on the planet, especially out of season, but nowhere was completely safe. Croatians knew that all too well. He set off at a run, speeding down the slope and onto the beach, skidding to a halt as he looked out to sea, hoping not to see a drowning person, a boat in distress or any of the other scenarios that flashed through his mind as he heard the anguished cry.

His prayer was granted. The only person in view was a woman standing on the edge of the sea, shouting out her pain to the birds and fish. He paused, uncertain. Whoever she was she clearly thought she was alone. She would probably be mortified to know that she been witnessed, but at the same time just walking away and leaving a fellow human being in such a state felt wrong. Damir swore softly. He wasn't so good at the touchy-feely people stuff. His ex-wife had made that all too clear.

To his utter relief, the woman stopped shouting before he intervened. She still stood with her back to him so he had no idea if she was laughing or crying, but she didn't look as if she was in any imminent danger: she wasn't wading into the waves or pulling at her hair. She just stood, slumped, unhappiness radiating from her almost palpably. He should just leave her to it, whatever *it* was. Damir took a step backwards. And as he did so his gaze snagged on the graceful, white villa overlooking the sea. He narrowed his eyes, looking from the villa to the woman.

He didn't recognise her, knew no one with long, honey-blonde hair, currently falling out of its makeshift bun. He didn't know any woman of that exact height and build, tall, curvy and toned, with long lean legs. She could be a tourist as a few did visit out of season, lured by the quiet promised by the island. But she wasn't staying at his hotel, hadn't eaten in his restaurant, and none of his apartments had been let, which left her with very few possible places to stay. One of which was staring him in the face.

Damir retreated quietly until he was sure he was out of earshot of the beach. He pulled his phone from his pocket and found the contact he needed. Less than two rings and the phone call was answered.

'Damir?' The voice was sleepy, as if woken by the call. Damir smiled wryly. His cousin liked to take things easy. The only thing he worked hard at was partying.

'Goran, did you have any passengers yesterday?'

'No, at least nobody new. Just the usual

Saturday marketeers. But I believe Igor had a late-night commission. An English girl, needed to be brought over from the mainland.'

Damir's pulse quickened. 'An English girl? Where is she staying?'

'You're best off speaking to Igor, but I think he had arranged a buggy to take her over to the villa at Fire Cove.'

'The villa?'

'Yeah, Marija's place. Igor said the girl is Josip's stepdaughter—he married an English woman a while back, that's why Marija always goes to England over Christmas. But he didn't get much more out of her. A looker he said, but pretty quiet. Why are you so interested anyway?'

'No reason,' Damir lied. He didn't want anyone, not even his cousin, to know how badly he wanted the villa. Not everyone on the island was happy with how much of the island's economy his family controlled. If word got out that he was trying to buy the villa—and with it the lucrative beach trade, he knew he would soon have competitors vying against him. They would be unlikely to be able to afford to outbid him, but they might put the price up. 'Like you say, she's a looker and it's not often pretty girls visit the island out of season.'

'If she's Josip's stepdaughter I guess that makes her one of us.'

'I guess that does. I'd better go make her welcome. Thanks.'

He pocketed his phone and stared back at the narrow sandy path leading to the beach. The one sandy beach on the whole of the island, one of the very few along this rocky coastline. Its perfect curve, fine white sand and gradual shelf made it a safe swimming spot, the tides predictable and gentle, a great place to learn to boat or paddle board or kayak. The sun hit early and continued to beam down until the spectacular sunset. No wonder it was a must-visit destination for the hundreds of thousands of visitors who visited the Dalmatian Riviera every year.

Most came as day trippers, but an increasing amount chose to stay on the island for a night or few, some for even a week, loving the feeling of exclusivity as the last boat pulled away. Damir owned the island's only hotel along with nearly all the apartments available for holiday lets, the island's best restaurant plus a harbourside café-bar, and he had a stake in several other businesses too. The ice-cream stall was his, the little local store and the bakery.

It was small fry compared to his investments in Dubrovnik itself and the rest of the Dalmatian Riviera, but Lokvar was where he was from, where his father and grandfather were from, and it was here that he had made his promise to make the Kozina name respected throughout the city, throughout the country. To achieve the dreams his father and grandfather had hatched throughout the years of repression and conflict. It was a promise that had cost him his marriage, but a promise he was well on the way to achieving.

If he could purchase the villa then his work here on Lokvar would be done. The owner of the villa—and more importantly, the land it stood on—owned the access to the beach, the land overlooking the famous bay, and had all the rights and means to capitalise on the tourists who visited there. Marija kept things simple; a modest B&B, a café-bar and a few sunbeds. Damir's plans were far more exciting. He could turn the bay into Croatia's premier resort. An island getaway. He just needed the villa and, with Josip, Marija's son, clearly settled in England, and Marija beginning to slow down, it had seemed that his time had come.

A grudging smile curved his lips. Trust Marija to make things complicated, saying she needed a year to think about it. With prices around Dubrovnik rocketing with every month and every film or TV series filmed in the scenic capital, a year could prove costly. Unless Damir could get the rest of her family onside...

He didn't know Josip himself. The older man had once been a close friend of Damir's own father, and with him had joined the volunteers tasked with defending Dubrovnik during the siege in the early nineties, but had left his island and country soon after, never to return, and the friendship had died. Any business with Josip would be impersonal, despite the age-old friendship between the families, conducted by lawyers. Unless he could get the stepdaughter to look favourably upon his bid.

She might be here just for a night, checking in on the family's property or for a holiday before the season swung into place. Either way time was of the essence. Damir hesitated, picturing again the girl's defeated pose, the raw hurt in her cry, then set his jaw. He had a job to do, and she might just be the key he needed. It was time to show her just how friendly the locals could be.

CHAPTER TWO

LILY'S THROAT WAS RAW, but for the first time in months she felt, if not free, lighter at least. The heavy grief and anger that seemed to continually cloak her in misery and darkness had lifted a little, allowing her to not just notice the warm morning sun but to feel it, the view refreshing her sore eyes.

Wincing at the pain in her throat, she dashed away a tear and took a shaky breath. This fresh start was exactly what she needed. Josip was, as usual, right. A new place, a new challenge and the opportunity to figure out who she was when all she had planned to be seemed futile.

It was daunting, but for the first time Lily felt a tingle of excitement at the challenge. She'd promised Izzy that she would live enough for the two of them, and finally she was making a start. For the next few months this was her workplace and this her work wardrobe instead of the constricting power suits and crippling heels, early morning commute and endless billable hours.

Her stomach rumbled, reminding her she had barely eaten the day before, but she couldn't bring herself to tear her gaze away from the beauty and tranquillity before her, feeling her battered soul start to repair with every rippling wave. She lingered, taking in strength from the sea, trying to summon up the resolve to walk the short but steep path to the tiny village, only to jump as a deep male voice spoke out from right behind her.

'Are you okay?'

Quickly spinning to face the speaker, Lily took a wary step back as she took in the man who had crept up so noiselessly behind her. Her hands tightened on her phone but whether she planned to use it to call for help or as an absurdly useless weapon she didn't yet know.

'I'm sorry,' the man continued in the same deep, gravelly voice, his Croatian accent as familiar to her as home. 'I didn't mean to frighten you, but you seem to be in distress. I just wanted to check that you're okay.'

Lily's panic ebbed as she noted that the expression in his dark eyes seemed sincere.

'Yes, thank you, I'm fine. Thank you,' she replied and did her best to summon a smile. 'It's very kind of you to check on me, but there's no need.' She held the rigid smile, expecting him to nod and move away, but he remained still, his dark eyes fixed on hers, his expression curious. How long had he been standing there? What had he heard? Enough to know to speak to her in English. Lily's cheeks heated and she tilted her chin, channelling as much poise and dignity as she could muster into her stance.

'I… Ah, I was just practising a healing ritual,' she said, semi-truthfully. Primal screaming was one of the many suggestions well-meaning friends and colleagues had suggested to her over the last three months: primal screaming, kickboxing, therapy, yoga both hot and cold, companion animals, poetry… Everyone seemed to know a way to heal her grief. But the truth was that Lily wasn't ready to heal. What if when the grief left her, Izzy went too? She wasn't ready to say goodbye. Not yet. Maybe not ever.

The man raised an eyebrow much to her reluctant admiration. She'd never been able to pull off that particular gesture although she had tried plenty of times in her teens. 'Healing ritual?'

'Apparently it gets rid of any negative toxins.'

His mouth quirked into a half-smile far more attractive than any smile had any right to be. 'And this is how you start every morning?'

'No, this was the first time. My home is in London and although Londoners are notorious for minding their own business, my neighbours would probably have something to say if I woke them up every morning in that fashion. But I thought I was alone here…' She put an emphasis on the word *alone* but the man didn't seem to notice. Instead, he held out a bronzed capable-looking hand.

'I'm Damir.'

Lily drew in a slow breath. Why couldn't he take the hint and just go away? But, she remembered, this was a small island, one with just three hundred full-time inhabitants. If she was going to spend the whole summer here, she would need to be civil to every one of those three hundred. After all, she was both a stranger and Marija's representative. Being civil, she supposed, included being polite to nosy men who seemingly couldn't take a hint.

Nosy and, if she was being honest, rather disturbingly attractive.

'Lily Woodhouse.' She made no move to take his hand and he casually dropped it to his side as if he hadn't even noticed her snub. Did nothing discombobulate him? Lily had never met anyone so seemingly at home in his own skin before. Tall, lean but with a quiet strength, Damir was just a few years older than she was, around thirty, she estimated. His jeans and short-sleeved white shirt were casual but exquisitely and expensively cut, showing off the breadth of his shoulders and muscled forearms and thighs. His dark hair was longer than she was used to, the alpha male city types she worked with favoured no-nonsense close crops and clean shaves, but Damir's chin was covered with dark morning stubble and his hair grazed his neck at the back, falling disarmingly onto his forehead, framing eyes so brown they were almost black. A firm chin, cheekbones cut sharper than a mountain ridge and a resolute mouth defined by a dangerously sexy dimple at the corner of his mouth, adding a boyishness to the handsome features, completed the undeniably appealing package.

Heat stirred low in her belly, as unwelcome as it was unexpected. The last thing Lily was interested in was dating, but there was an edgy attractiveness to him that even her tired body reluctantly responded to.

Damir's smile widened. 'Welcome to Lokvar, Lily Woodhouse. Will you be staying with us for long?'

Lily hesitated, but her job here was no secret and the sooner the word was out who she was and why she was here the better. 'For the summer,' she said. 'I'm looking after the villa over there. Marija's villa.'

'So you must be Josip's daughter?'

'Yes.' She didn't need to correct the assumption and add in the 'step'—she couldn't imagine loving any actual father more than she loved Josip.

'We all miss Marija, she is very respected. I hope she is okay?' The dark eyes glowed with sincerity.

Some of Lily's tension melted at the thought of her voluble grandmother. 'She had a wonderful few months in New Zealand. Her pictures are amazing, one minute she's in Hobbiton, the next whale watching. She's in the States now, planning a trip to Nashville.'

'And she's left you in charge? Quite a responsibility.' His gaze sharpened. 'Are you used to working in hospitality?'

'I'm a lawyer.' Lily said, bristling a little at the unwanted interrogation. 'But I waitressed a lot through school and university, I'm used to dealing with people.'

'A lawyer? Your firm must be very accommodating to allow you to take the summer off.'

What was with all the questions? Lily folded her arms and took a step back. 'I'm on a sabbatical.' That was what they were calling it anyway. Her boss had refused to accept the resignation she had sent in six weeks after Izzy's funeral. She was marked for partner one day, those fourteen-to-sixteen-hour days leading her along a path she had thought she wanted. Had worked towards tirelessly, spending her life in the library while her peers were clubbing, determined not to make her mother's mistakes.

'Take some time,' Priya had said with uncharacteristic kindness. 'Think about it before you do anything irrevocable. Your job is open for six months. We'd hate to lose you, Lily, you are one of our brightest and best. I have great hopes for you.' Once those words were all Lily had wanted to hear. Now they were as meaningless as the glass and metal apartment with its views over London she'd been so excited to move into, or her wardrobe of expensive suits and designer shoes.

She glanced towards the villa, angling away from Damir in a clear gesture that she was ready to finish the conversation. 'It's nice meeting you, Damir, but I really need to find some breakfast before Ana arrives.

I didn't get a chance to stock up yesterday as my flight was delayed.'

'In that case,' Damir said smoothly, 'you must allow me to buy you some breakfast. As a way to welcome you to the island. Please, it would be entirely my pleasure.'

Damir leaned back in his chair and surreptitiously surveyed Lily through his sunglasses as she dipped her bread in olive oil before topping it with creamy feta cheese. After her initial wariness she seemed to have started to relax, helped no doubt by the excellent coffee and platter of bread, cheese and olives along with the small pastries and homemade jam he'd presented her with after seating her at a table overlooking the harbour.

It had taken some of his best persuasive methods and all his charm to persuade the clearly suspicious English girl to accept his offer of breakfast. But once he'd mentioned that only one island café was open at this time of year, and that he just happened to be the owner, she had thawed a little and finally accepted his offer, although she had said little on the short but steep walk across the island to the village, clearly still pre-occupied with whatever had provoked her distress on the beach.

He didn't mind her silence, it gave him time to work out how to turn this unexpected opportunity to his advantage. Marija had made it clear to him that she wouldn't consider his offer to buy the villa until she had spent a year away. He had planned to spend that time ensuring an irresistible proposal was ready for her return, and that everything was in place to start moving the second she signed the contract. Lily hadn't featured in his plans. After all, it was only a few days since he'd heard rumours that Josip's English daughter was coming to look after the villa.

But here she was, a pale, solemn girl with pain in her eyes and a smile that looked as if it was pasted on. There was a story there, but Damir wasn't interested in stories. What he *was* interested in was finding out just what Marija's long-term plans were and if this girl figured in them. If she did, he needed to make some readjustments. And if not, if she was only here for the summer, then maybe he could get her to see that his offer was the best thing for Marija. For the island. Which meant turning the charm up, breaking the silence and befriending her. After all, so far she knew no one here. He could show her around, make himself indispensable. It wouldn't exactly be a hardship, she was a pretty girl.

'How's your breakfast?' Not the most original of questions but he had to start a conversation somehow. Lily looked up, her expression a little confused as if she had forgotten where she was and who she was with. And then she smiled, her face transformed from pretty to extraordinarily beautiful by the gesture, and Damir felt a flickering of desire tighten his stomach. His clasp tightened on his cup. He didn't need or want feelings to complicate business. And this was all about business. What else was there?

'This coffee is the best coffee I've ever had in my entire life,' Lily said, taking another sip. 'I've been to so many hipster cafés with menus showcasing literally hundreds of coffees from all over the world, boasting about the origin and roasting process and the rarity of the beans, and not one cup has come close to this.'

'Croatians take their coffee very seriously.' Damir picked up his own cup and inhaled the satisfyingly bitter steam. 'If you're going to spend the summer here, then this is probably the most important thing you need to know.'

'Marija said that most of her guests are English or German or American, but she does get a fair number of Croatians as well. I hope Ana knows how to make coffee because I don't think my barista talents are up to scratch.'

'Just make it strong,' Damir advised her. 'That's the most important thing. Croatians may forgive a less than perfect cup, but they won't forgive a weak one.'

'I'll remember that, thank you.' Lily pushed her plate away with another of those breath-taking smiles. The flickering of desire intensified and this time Damir didn't rush to quench it, much as he knew he should. 'And thank you for breakfast. That was absolute delicious, I needed it much more than I realised. Yesterday was a very long day, and the last few months have been… Anyway, I feel much more ready to get started now.' She leaned back, looking around her, eyes wide. 'What an amazing view and right on the harbour. It's an incredible position. You must be the first port of call when the ferries and boats arrive.'

That was why his grandfather had chosen to situate the café here, of course, and Damir had learned the lesson well: his hotel and restaurant, like the café, were carefully positioned to ensure proximity to the small village whilst ensuring guests had the best views on the island—apart from Marija's villa. 'First and last port of call. There is no better spot to while away half an hour waiting for a boat.'

'Have your family always owned it?'

'My grandfather opened it—he was the village baker, but always wanted to own a restaurant. He passed it onto my father and then to me.'

'And what about the bakery?'

'I own that too.'

Lily raised her eyebrows. 'Quite the island monopoly you have there.'

'You could say that,' Damir said noncommittally. Of course, many people *did* say exactly that.

'What's it like?' Lily leaned forward, her hands clasped around the coffee cup. 'Living in such a small place, seeing the same faces every single day, with the sea between you and the next town? Does it get claustrophobic?' There was an intensity to the question Damir couldn't interpret. He got the impression that Lily Woodhouse was running away from something.

'Claustrophobic? How could it feel claustrophobic when the sky stretches all around, when you look out onto the endless sea? But, no, island life isn't for everyone. A few are born here and never leave, others return after time away and some go as soon as they can and never come back. But people here are like people anywhere, there are those who gossip, there are those who like to stir up trouble, those who don't pull their weight. But there's nowhere else like it. Of course, we all have our own boats so we can escape from each other when we need to.'

She laughed, but the shadows were back in her eyes. 'And do you? Escape?'

'Ah, well, I actually only live here part of the time. I have a villa in Dubrovnik, I run most of my business from there...'

'In Dubrovnik? There's more, then, than the café and bakery monopoly?'

'Some holiday lets,' he said smoothly. Damir wasn't sure why he was hiding the bulk of his business from Lily. After all, Marija had a very good idea of his situation, all the island did, it was hardly a secret. But he had a sense that it would be easier to get Lily to trust him, to advocate for him, if she saw him as a small-time businessman. Maybe, if she knew just how real his island monopoly actually was, with the hotels and restaurants and the apartments in Dubrovnik, the villas along the coastline, she would be as uneasy about his desire to also own the coveted access onto the beach as her grandmother was.

There was another reason behind his decision to downplay his wealth, although he barely liked to admit it even to himself. Money had changed how people saw him, changed his standing in the community, in the city. Since his divorce, he'd been the target of local socialites, interested not in him but in the wealth he'd accumulated and the covetable real estate he owned.

He had no problem with the unacknowledged chasm between himself and his former peers and he certainly didn't mind the attention of the city's wealthiest and most eligible young women. But there was a simple pleasure sitting in the morning sun, enjoying getting to know a pretty girl who had no preconceptions about him. A pleasure he hadn't enjoyed for a very long time. Not since Kata.

He pushed the memory of his ex-wife away, glad of the reminder that he should never mix business with pleasure. Attractive as she was, Lily clearly had secrets of her own and history had taught him that his dreams and complicated women did not mix. If he married again he would choose one of the socialites, a woman who understood how marriage at his level worked. Someone who in return for a lavish lifestyle would raise his family, be a consummate hostess and need nothing else from him.

'Thank you again for breakfast.' Lily

pushed back her chair and stood up. 'You must let me repay you when we're open for business.'

'It was my pleasure, no repayment necessary.' Although he would take her up on the offer. It would be an excellent way to further the acquaintance. 'What are your plans for the rest of the day?'

'Explore a little and then I had better go and familiarise myself with the villa before Ana gets here so I don't look like too much of an idiot. I also need to put my first order together—Marija says if I email it to the supermarket they deliver it to the ferry and I just need to meet the ferry with a golf cart. Much cheaper than the local shop. Although maybe I shouldn't have said that.' She clapped a hand over her mouth, eyes bright with a laughing apology. 'You probably own the local shop too, don't you?'

'Everyone on the island orders off the mainland.' Damir neatly sidestepped the question of the shop's ownership. 'But they're very grateful for the shop when the weather is stormy or they've run out of milk for their morning coffee. It was nice to meet you, Lily. Let me know if you need any help with anything. I'd love to show you around sometime, you should take the opportunity to explore while you're here and I am a wonderful tour guide, or so I've been told.'

He also stood up and held out his hand, and after a tiny hesitation she took it, her clasp smooth and warm. His pulse jumped at the contact, electricity zinging up his arm, and it was all he could do not to drop her hand and jump back. What was that about?

True, he had been working ridiculous hours lately even by his standards so maybe this reaction was a sign he should indulge in one of the short, no-strings relationships he had occasionally embarked on since his divorce. He released her hand, his heart still hammering.

'That's very kind of you, but I'm not sure how much time I'll have for sightseeing. Thank you again—and I am sorry for this morning. I forgot how small the island actually is so no more morning rituals on the beach for me. Anyway, as it's a small island, I'm sure I'll see you again.' And with another quick smile she was off, hurrying back along the harbourside to the narrow road that crisscrossed the island.

Frowning, Damir watched her go. She'd jumped back from his offer to take her out as if it were a marriage proposal. It was a long time since he'd been turned down by a woman. Still, it wasn't yet June and summer was a long season on Lokvar. He had plenty of time to befriend the English girl. By the end of the summer he'd have her exactly where he wanted her—on his side. After all, this was business and that was an area where he always won out in the end.

CHAPTER THREE

'I CAN'T BELIEVE that in a few days' time
the villa will be full of guests.' Lily shook
a pillow vigorously. 'I have no idea how
we'll be ready on time. Thank goodness
you already took care of hiring the staff
and they'll be here tomorrow to help us.'

She placed the pillow with exaggerated
care on the bed she was making up and
grinned at Ana, Josip's cousin and Marija's right hand woman. Every summer Ana
left her home in the capital, Zagreb, to return to the island of her birth and help run
the B&B—and as Lily realised less than
hour after meeting her she was a fount of
all knowledge about everyone and everything on Lokvar.

Several times Lily had tried to get up the
courage to ask her aunt about Damir but
couldn't quite find the words. His offer to

show her around was probably just common courtesy—but there had been something more than mere politeness in his eyes, a curious intentness she couldn't decipher.

Neither could she work out her own reaction to him. That jolting physical reaction, unlike anything she had ever felt before on a first meeting, unexpected—and not exactly unpleasant—heat coursing through her body. It wasn't like her. She always, always took relationships slowly; compatibility, then liking, then attraction. That was the safe, the sensible thing to do.

But, then again, wasn't she here to be a little less safe, a little less sensible? She picked up another pillow and pummelled it extra hard, glad to take out her uncertainty on the inanimate object.

'I had no idea just how much there was to do,' she continued, hoping to banish persistent thoughts of dark, dark eyes from her mind. 'All the floors to scrub and polish, the curtains to wash and iron, and that's not even considering outside. I've started the weeding, but all the paintwork still needs freshening. It's a good thing I didn't assume that spending the summer here on Lokvar was a chance to take things easy, imagine how disappointed I would be! I've barely had two minutes to sit in the sun, and I'm not sure that's going to change any time soon.'

What she didn't say, tried not to think, was that it suited her to keep so busy, it stopped her from thinking. Stopped her from missing Izzy, from remembering her promise, a promise she had no idea how to actually keep. How did she change the deeply ingrained habits of a lifetime, start living for today instead of planning for tomorrow? Yes, she had taken leave from her work to come here, but what next?

The way things were going she was going to be too busy to work out how to be spontaneous anyway. But if she didn't follow through then not only was she breaking a promise but she'd have failed. Only Izzy had known just how much Lily hated to fail. So somehow she was going to just get on with it. Be spontaneous. Have fun. Live enough for the lost years of hard work and planning, for Izzy's lost future.

'Don't worry about the paintwork. Luka

can take care of that.' Ana took the battered pillow from Lily and placed it beside its fellow, straightening the sheet's edge as she did so. Immediately the room looked made up, crisp and clean. Ana had magic in her fingers, a way of making everything look just so. A talent Lily knew she didn't have a chance of emulating.

'We'd best make use of that lazy son of mine while we can. Once tourists start turning up and wanting to hire sunbeds and order drinks he'll be otherwise occupied. I hope I haven't made a mistake bringing him here this summer, I don't want him to waste his time lounging outside, flirting with pretty tourists.'

'I'm sure poor Luka will do nothing of the sort,' protested Lily. 'Look at how much help he's been yesterday and this morning.'

'When he looked up from his books, that was.' Ana might sound annoyed but she couldn't hide the proud glow in her eyes. Her other children had all grown up and moved out long ago. Luka, in his second year at the local university, had been a surprise baby, born once his siblings had reached teenhood and quite clearly the apple of his doting mother's eyes.

'You can't have it both ways,' Lily said. 'Either he's too studious or all he wants to do is ogle tourists, pick one.'

'I'm sure he is quite capable of doing both,' Ana said darkly, and picked up the pillow to give it another hard shake.

A warm glow filled Lily. It was nice, this comradely routine. At the high-powered corporate law firm she'd worked for since she'd left Oxford, there was no such thing as chitchat. Everyone was competitive, everybody out for the main advantage and every word a weapon. She hadn't enjoyed gossip at work like this since she and Izzy had worked together in a local café during sixth form.

She turned around to survey the bedroom, the first one readied for the expected guests. Marija's villa didn't labour under any boutique hotel pretensions. It was simple, clean and homely and Lily loved it. The floors were wooden and covered in brightly coloured rugs, the walls a bright fresh white, hung with Croatian seascapes. The furniture was unpretentious but well made: comfortable sofas heaped with cushions, iron bedsteads and soft white linen. There was no on-site gym, no pool, but there were stunning views from every window and it was less than two minutes from the front door to the edge of the sea.

A buzzing noise filled the room and Lily darted to the window to see a golf cart cresting the hill that led to the village. 'Ooh, I wonder what that is?' She couldn't get over the charming novelty of receiving her groceries by golf cart once they'd arrived on that morning's ferry.

'I thought we'd received today's order,' Ana said.

'We did but maybe we forgot something. I'll go check.' Lily sprang down the stairs, out of the open front door and down the small stone flight of stairs leading onto a wide paved terrace where she almost barrelled into the bronzed young man who delivered orders from the ferry.

'Sorry,' she gasped. 'I thought I'd save you a trip. Oh…' She stopped as she realised that, instead of the expected bag of groceries, he held a gorgeous bouquet of flowers. 'Are these for us? *Hvala.*' Thank you was of the very few words of Croatian she could manage.

She took the huge bouquet, barely able to see over the top of the colourful blooms and, much more carefully than she had exited the villa, returned to the hallway where Ana was waiting for her.

'Aren't they beautiful?' Lily carefully placed them on the perfectly polished reception desk. 'They must be from Mum and Josip. How thoughtful. That is, if they are for me?' She looked guiltily at the older woman. 'Of course, they could be for you.'

'For me?' Ana's laugh echoed melodiously around the hallway. 'Who would be sending me flowers like that? If it was my husband I'd be immediately suspicious about what he was up to.'

'I'm sure he still sends you flowers sometimes. Let's see.' Lily extracted the envelope tucked into the side of the flowers and opened it, staring at the words in disbelief, heat infusing her cheeks as she did so. 'Oh! They're not from Mum after all. How peculiar.'

She read the card again, not sure she'd

taken it in properly the first time, but there was no change in the words, written in decisive yet elegant script.

Dear Lily,
Good luck for the start of the season.
I hope to see you at the island party tomorrow.
If you've changed your mind about that personal tour just let me know.
Damir

Lily's cheeks heated even further as she handed Ana the card and watched her read it, her thinly plucked eyebrows almost comically high. Ana whistled long and low as she gave the card back to Lily.

'Damir Kozina,' she said slowly, drawing out every syllable. Lily couldn't tell if her tone was admiring or admonishing. 'I didn't know you two were acquainted.'

'Hardly,' protested Lily. 'I ran into him just before you arrived and he bought me breakfast, nothing more exciting than that.' She looked again at the flowers, bright and cheerful and clearly expensive. 'Certainly nothing exciting enough to warrant flowers like these. Maybe he's just being nice...' she finished doubtfully.

'Damir? Nice?' Ana gave a snort of laughter. 'I've never known him do anything if there isn't something in it for him. You must have made quite an impression.'

'I probably did,' Lily admitted. 'He caught me at a weak moment. These flowers are probably a pity gift more than anything else. I bet he thinks I'm not going to last the first week of having to deal with actual people.'

'If you say so,' Ana said. 'Be careful, though, he has quite a reputation.'

'Oh?' Here was the chance she'd been waiting for. So why wasn't she jumping straight in with questions? Luckily Ana continued before she could think of something that sounded suitably disinterested.

'He's been a bit of a playboy since his divorce. High-maintenance girls from the mainland if my sources are right, and they usually are. I wouldn't have said you were his type, I've never known him go after tourists or islanders before. I guess we'll see at the party. You'll be turning all the single girls green if Damir *is* interested in you. Half the seasonal staff only take jobs here in the hope of snaring him.'

Lily couldn't help but feel a twinge— well, more than a twinge if she was being honest—of curiosity at the information, but something more pressing had to be dealt with. This wasn't the first time the harbourside party that kicked off the season in Lokvar had been mentioned over the last few days. It was clearly quite an occasion, but the thought of spending an evening with a lot of strangers, bound to ask about why she was here, was a terrifying thought. 'Oh, yes.' Lily turned away, aiming for nonchalant. 'The party. I'm not sure that I'm going to go.'

'Not go?' Ana said, her voice incredulous. 'But, Lily, everybody goes. It's our last chance to relax and enjoy ourselves before the summer starts.'

'Parties aren't really my thing,' Lily said. 'Besides, this is the island's party, for the people who live here. I'm just as much a visitor as the tourists and I don't speak a word of Croatian. I'd probably just make people uncomfortable, hanging around not knowing anyone and not able to join in, needing everyone to translate all the time.'

'You may have noticed, everybody speaks English.' Ana put her hands on her hips. 'And you are Marija's granddaughter, which makes you one of us. Your grandmother never misses a party, in fact she is usually one of the last to leave. If you are here looking after things for her then it's your duty to represent her. We've got a long and busy season ahead of us, Lily, you have to grab your fun where you can.'

The protest died on Lily's lips. Hadn't she just been wondering where to start with her *live for the moment* project and here she was, failing at the first hurdle. Was it the thought of a whole party full of strangers that daunted her—or the knowledge that Damir would be there possibly looking for her? Or, worse, not looking for her and flirting with some heiress.

'Maybe you're right. I'll think about it,' Lily said. 'I promise.'

'Make sure you do. Don't shut yourself away, Lily.' Ana gave her hand a quick squeeze before bustling away to berate Luka for taking a quick break.

Lily slowly made her way back upstairs, leaving the flowers on the reception desk. Beautiful as they were, they would dominate her small room, be a constant reminder of Damir and the way she'd reacted to him, the way a tingle had shot up her arm when he'd touched her, the way his half-smile had made her want to reach out and touch that unlikely dimple. She'd done her best to put him out of her mind, but when she'd walked to the shop yesterday and seen a tall, lean man in sunglasses and an expensive-looking shirt, an unequivocal quiver of expectation had rippled through her, only to turn to disappointment when he'd turned out to be a complete stranger.

She paused, torn between returning to work and taking some time out, before heading up another floor to her small attic bedroom. The room was sparsely furnished: a bed, a small wardrobe and a dressing table, a rug on the floor. She had brought little with her, and the room was almost devoid of anything personal except for a framed picture on the dressing table. Lily picked it up, swallowing as she did so.

She didn't really need to look at it, she

knew exactly what she'd see, could have described every detail down to the flowers in the background and the colour of the subjects' brightly painted toenails. But she studied it, as if answers could be found in the laughing face of the two girls in the photo.

The girls were around sixteen, posing dramatically in the back garden of Lily's parents' small terraced house in Ealing. They were both dressed up, Lily in a floor-length dress of a deep blue that matched her eyes and made her blonde hair gleam golden in the sun, the neckline and waist-line sparkling with tiny crystals, the same crystals studding her elaborate updo. Izzy, disdaining the traditional as usual, had gone for a vintage Fifties look in a vibrant red polka dot that suited her curves and wild, dark curls.

Lily couldn't look at the photo without remembering the intense concentration it had taken for Izzy to outline her eyes with a perfect cat flick, or the at least four coats of mascara it had taken her to achieve the big-eyed look she'd wanted. They looked so innocent, so full of life, convinced everything they wanted lay before them. If they'd known just how little time they really had, would they have changed everything? Spent more time living, less time planning? Been bolder?

'I can't remember the last time I went to a party without you,' Lily said out loud. 'Who will I talk to? Who will understand my signal when I've had enough and want to leave or want to ditch the guy who won't take a hint?' Or give her the thumbs up if she didn't want to ditch the guy but needed a second opinion?

Lily carefully placed the framed photo back onto the dressing table and started to turn away, but the sunlight fell on Izzy's face, and she stopped. 'What?' Lily asked. 'You think I should go? You were the brave one, not me. You led I followed, you know that.'

She waited, half expecting an answer, and dashed away a tear, angry at her foolishness. 'What more can I do? I know I promised it would all be different. I promised no more planning, no more existing. I promised I'd live enough for us both. Well, I'm here. Look. Not in an office, not in the apartment or the gym. I'm actually abroad. And, yes, I haven't seen much of abroad yet and, yes, I have been working since I got here but it's a start.'

Another pause then Lily heaved a sigh, one so deep it hurt her already weary heart. 'You're right. I should have said yes to the offer to explore. I should say yes more often, not hide behind, well, I'm not sure what I hide behind now you're not here. He was hot, don't you think he was hot? Not like those corporate finance guys I dated or even like the hipster Silicon Valley tycoon wannabes you used to meet. He didn't look like a treadmill pounder to me, more like someone who isn't afraid to get his hands dirty.'

She sat down on the bed, then flopped down onto her pillow, lying back to stare up at the ceiling fan, remembering the way Damir had held her gaze, the warmth in his eyes. He'd asked her out, sent her flowers and she was still planning to hide back at the villa?

Ana had said he was a playboy. That settled it. Lily was not a playboy's type. Too sensible, too busy, too boring.

But not here. Here she was new, different, trying to be impulsive. And wouldn't a playboy be a good person to be impulsive with? Lily wasn't looking for love or marriage, but a summer away should include a little romance, surely? Armed with foreknowledge she'd be in no danger of falling for Damir's practised charms, but maybe she could enjoy a no-strings flirtation?

'Okay, you win. As usual. I will go to the party and I will try to flirt with the hot guy, and if he offers to take me to explore again I'll accept. Satisfied?'

Lily sat up and glared at the photo. Obviously it was a trick of the light, but for one moment she could have sworn Izzy gave her a nod of approval.

CHAPTER FOUR

DAMIR DOUBLE-CHECKED THE mooring ropes one last time before lightly springing off his boat onto the long wooden jetty, his chest clenching as he took in the carnival-like atmosphere.

The wide paved promenade that fronted Lokvar's small and only village hummed with a throng of excited, chattering people, many of whom were dressed up for the occasion. Fairy lights were strung around every available tree, sign or post and, although it was not yet dusk, shone brightly. The rich smells of grilled meat and vegetables permeated the air and the unmistakable heavy rock sounds of the island's one and only band rang out, a makeshift dance floor roped off to minimise the risk of one of the overexcited children already jumping up and down falling into the shallow sea.

Lokvar village spanned half of the island's wide main bay. The brightly coloured, thick-walled fishermen's cottages were now shops and apartments catering to tourists, the residents having moved inland to live in newer, more convenient villas and apartments. But for festivals everyone congregated here by the sea. Damir knew every single person drinking and laughing on the harbourside—and they all knew him.

His chest tightened further. Truth was he hadn't enjoyed an island party since the season end celebration seven years ago when his ex-wife Kata had turned and walked away, ending their marriage as she did so. No, before that, since his wealth had started to divide him from the people he had grown up with. He only attended because he sponsored it. Because it was expected.

He set his jaw grimly. He had only had two failures in his life. The death of his father and the collapse of his marriage. He would not tolerate a third. Tonight he would find, flatter and woo the English girl and find out Marija's long-term plans. Fulfilling his father's plan to develop Fire Cove would help assuage some of his guilt over how he had let him down in life.

But beneath the determination he was aware of an entirely different emotion—anticipation. Not the expected anticipation of long-awaited business success but anticipation of seeing the English girl—Lily—again.

He couldn't remember the last time such a short meeting had had such an effect on him—and he had no idea why. She was pretty enough, especially when she unleashed that breath-taking smile, but she hadn't said much during their one meeting, and of course when he had first seen her she had been doing a fine impersonation of some kind of Bacchanal naiad, yelling out to sea. Not quite the cool, poised, confidence displayed by the women he usually chose for the safe, short-term relationships he preferred.

But the lurking sadness in her eyes, the sense of regret and pain had called to him. After all, they mirrored his own. Hopefully tonight he'd be able to get her out of his brain once and for all and concentrate on what really mattered. The villa.

Damir squared his shoulders and strolled off the jetty, joining the nearest gathering, radiating all the confidence due to the owner of half the island. The man who sponsored tonight's festivities and employed most of the guests.

'Damir, finally!'

'There's a drink here with your name on it, my friend. Well, you did pay for it!'

Immediately friends and relatives, most of whom worked for him, surrounded him, bombarding him with the gossip from the evening so far, handing him a gratefully received pint of beer. For a moment it was as if he had stepped back in time to when his father had been alive, Kata by his side, and he was still—just—one of the gang. Occasionally he missed this comradeship and ease, so different from the politely cut-throat friendships found in the boardrooms, golf clubs and highbrow functions attended by Dubrovnik's old aristocratic and new moneyed classes to which he now belonged. Part of him would have liked to stay right here, reverted to being the old

Damir for one night only. But as always he had work to do.

Work that would start once Lily arrived. The flowers were just the first step. Tonight he would dazzle her with attention, invite her out onto his boat, woo her. Play his cards right and the English girl would be putty in his hands, ready to be moulded into the perfect ally.

Taking a sip of beer, Damir looked around, hoping to glimpse a flash of honey-blonde hair. His earlier anticipation ramped up, humming through him, every nerve hyperaware of every smell, sound and taste, from the rhythm of the band to the salt permeating the air. He took a breath, willing the adrenaline to slow.

A hush fell over the group and Damir realised his friends were looking at something—or someone—behind him with a mixture of curiosity and admiration. Hair prickled on the back of his neck. She was here, he could feel it. Turning slowly, he inhaled, a long, deep breath of appreciation. Lily and Ana were walking slowly down the winding, hilly path that bisected the island, chatting casually as they did so.

Ana, like most of the islanders, had dressed up in a dress and heels but Lily was more simply dressed in jeans and a silky cream camisole top, her long blonde hair loose, cascading way past her shoulders and moving in time with her stride. She wore little make-up but her cheeks were pink, potentially with embarrassment as nearly everyone had stopped to look at the newcomer in their midst. She tilted her chin defiantly and her eyes blazed with purpose. Damir's pulse began to beat loudly. She looked magnificent.

Barely aware of his friends' comments and sniggers, Damir stepped away from the group and walked slowly over to greet her as she finally descended the last few steps of the path.

'I'm so glad you made it, Lily,' he said, and smiled at her companion. 'It's lovely to see you, Ana, welcome back to Lokvar. I hope your family are well.'

Ana looked from Damir to Lily, her smile knowing. 'Everyone is fine, thank you. How is your mother?'

'She's good. I'll tell her that you were asking after her.'

'I was hoping she'd be here. It's been a long time since I saw her.'

'Since she remarried she prefers to stay on the mainland.' His mother had always maintained that if his father had had his heart attack in Dubrovnik, he'd have reached the hospital on time. She hadn't returned to Lokvar since. Or forgiven Damir for not working that day as his father had wanted.

That was fine, he didn't want her forgiveness. After all, he couldn't forgive himself.

Ana nodded. 'Well, give her my best.'

'I will. Enjoy the party.' Damir turned to Lily. 'It's nice to see you again, Lily.'

For a brief second an entire reel of emotions passed over Lily's face. Damir saw uncertainty and worry flicker there, before they disappeared as if they'd never been as she tilted her chin and smiled at him. 'Thank you for the flowers. I should buy you a drink to say thank you.'

'Not necessary, the bar is free tonight. But, please, join me?'

He noted the barely perceptible hesitation before she answered. 'That would be lovely.'

'Great, the bar's this way. Have a good evening,' he added politely to Ana, before leading Lily over to one of the outdoor bars that had been set up for the evening. 'What would you like? Both the beer and wine are brewed locally, and I can recommend both.'

'In that case a glass of white wine, please.'

Damir was aware of being surreptitiously watched by at least half of the village as he procured a glass of white wine for Lily and a top-up of his own beer. He steered her towards an empty table, set aside from the rest, and placed the drinks on it.

'Thank you,' she said, as he pulled out her seat for her. 'And thank you again for the flowers, they're beautiful.'

'You're welcome. I wanted to mark the start of your first season. I know how hectic these weeks are even for people who do it year after year.'

'It has been crazy, although luckily I have Ana.' Lily shook her head ruefully. 'To be honest, she could run the whole place single-handedly. I'm pretty sure I'm more of a hindrance than a help.'

'I'm sure that's not true,' Damir protested, and Lily laughed.

'Oh, it is. I know she would deny it, she's far too nice, but she has to waste half her time showing me how to do things that are second nature to her.' She grimaced. 'In fact, the last couple of days have been a rude awakening. Quite a dent to my ego.'

'In what way?' Damir was, despite himself, intrigued. Lily was like a different woman. Last time they had sat here overlooking the sea she had been withdrawn, thoughtful, but tonight she sparkled with life. He'd been prepared to lead the conversation, to draw her out, not to find himself amused at her playful self-deprecation. Far from being wrong-footed, he found himself leaning in, fascinated.

'Okay, I appreciate how big-headed this sounds but I've always prided myself on being good at most things. I like to succeed. But it turns out being able to follow a recipe adequately does not equip me for a role in a commercial kitchen and my washing-up is not of a high enough standard for the chef. I only speak one language compared to Ana's four—four!—and so she will have to do most of the front of house and the bookings as well as manage the staff.

'And just when I think I've been really useful and cleaned something properly or made up a bedroom perfectly, I see her surreptitiously tidying up after me because I missed a corner.' Lily took a gulp of her wine. 'It's all been very lowering. My ambitions have shrunk to one thing only—to make a bed that Ana approves of. If only my manager could see me now.'

'Are you regretting choosing Lokvar for your sabbatical?'

It was a slightly flippant question, one in keeping with the lightness of the conversation. Damir was expecting Lily to brush it away with a comment about spending a summer abroad or the beauty of the island but instead she sat back and sipped her wine thoughtfully, clearly considering her answer.

'No,' she said at last. 'Obviously it's really lovely to see Marija's home in person, I've heard so much about it over the last few years. And it's been good to be so busy, even if I am a little bit ineffectual. I'm learning new skills and, more importantly, I'm learning how to get a sense of fulfilment from a small job well done and that's good for me. I'm usually always ten steps ahead, I don't allow myself the time to enjoy the moment and that's something I need to change. But mostly it's been good to get away from London and the office and start to think about what it's all really about.'

'It?'

'Life.'

Damir wasn't sure he'd heard her properly. 'Life?'

She nodded, eyes focussed on something or someone far away, as if she were half somewhere else. 'Life. I made a vow, to start living properly. I came here to get away from the sixteen-hour days and no social life and the intensity, but I know me, it's easy to fall back into bad habits, especially when there's the B&B to run and there's always something to do.

'So I've promised myself that I must do one spontaneous thing a day to try and break the cycle. But then I find that I am beginning to plan even that! I find it so uncomfortable to try and go with the flow.

And then I feel like I'm failing and I'm back to where I started. Promising myself I'll do better, be better.' She stopped then, cheeks pink. 'I am so sorry. I am so bad at this.'

'This?'

'Small talk. I am really out of practice— not that I was ever really good at it. You must think I am utterly crazy, shouting at the sea one day, yakking on about trying to be spontaneous the next.'

'I'm thinking,' Damir said slowly, 'that you're not like anybody else I know.'

'I'm sure that's true. You must be dying to get back to your friends and tell them all about the crazy English girl. Honestly, please, there is no need to be polite. I'll go find Ana. Thank you for the drink.'

'I'm not being polite,' Damir said, putting up a hand to stay her as she half rose from her seat. 'I'm right where I want to be.'

He would have said those exact words anyway, but to his surprise he realised they were the truth.

'That's very kind of you, but I'm not sure I believe you.' Lily covered her face with her hands for a second. 'What would Izzy say to me? No, I know exactly what she'd say, that I'm not fit to even conduct a light flirtation unsupervised. And she'd be right.'

Damir stilled, all intent to laugh disappearing, his whole body on high alert. He fought to keep his tone light. 'A flirtation? Is that what we're doing?'

Lily could feel her cheeks get hotter and hotter. She wanted to turn away, but was trapped by Damir's dark gaze. She couldn't tell if he was amused or horrified by her gaucheness. Probably both.

But it wasn't amusement or horror she could see in his eyes. Instead there was a flash of something more primal, almost predatory. A shiver snaked down her spine as she finally looked away, grabbing her wine glass and focussing on it as if it held the elixir of life.

'I…'

Possible get-out clauses flashed through her mind. She could say she'd meant *hypothetically*, try to laugh the awkward words off or, preferred option, simply run away.

But, she could hear Izzy say, *why not just own it?* Wasn't that what she was here to do? Flirt? Be spontaneous?

'Maybe not in any recognised sense of the word, but, yes, flirting with you was tonight's planned spontaneous decision.' She forced herself to sit back and sip her wine as if she were the confident woman she pretended to be. 'After all, you are the only person away from the B&B I have met so far and you *did* offer to show me around.'

'I did.' His gaze intensified. 'And I meant it.'

'Good.' She fought to keep her voice steady. 'Because I'd like to accept.'

'Good,' he echoed, and she could hear the smile in his voice. 'I wouldn't claim to be a master tour guide, but...' his smile turned wolfish and her insides molten '... I haven't had any complaints so far.'

Lily would bet a great deal he hadn't, not when he smiled with that particular intent, allowed his hair to fall broodingly across his brow, rolled up his sleeves to show bronzed, strong forearms, corded with muscle, folded his hands to show off his long, strong, capable fingers. She dragged her gaze up to meet his, lingering on the sensual tilt of his mouth as she did so.

'And what did you have in mind?' She tossed her hair back as she lounged back, glass in hand. 'I'm a lawyer, remember. I don't enter into any kind of agreement without clarity and a full perusal of the small print and sub-clauses.' Lawyer? Right now she was an actress. But she couldn't deny that now she'd started she was enjoying being someone else. Enjoying cutting loose from the confines of her rigid life.

'No small print. We spend time together. You set the limits. If you're uncomfortable say so and we stop.'

Why did she get the feeling he wasn't just talking about a walk around Dubrovnik?

'And when were you thinking?' Lily was aware that she was leaning towards him, that her gaze held his with coy challenge, that her voice was breathier than normal— and that hair toss was most unlike her. The atmosphere was charged, as if millions of pheromones were dancing around them, turning every word into a seduction, every look into a dance step.

'There's no time like the present.'

Lily swallowed, her throat dry. The game had got suddenly all too real and she had to decide whether she was really ready to play. What would be the harm in saying yes? She might make a fool of herself, even more than she already had, but she couldn't hide for ever. Not if she was going to keep her promise to Izzy and try living, not existing.

Lily didn't know what awaited her at the end of the summer, whether she would return to London, to her expensive sterile and lonely flat and her well paid soulless job and try for more balance, or whether she would make a more profound change. But she did know that if she didn't seize the chance to try living a different way, she would add to her already too heavy list of regrets.

'I guess not. So where do we start?'

'Have you properly explored the island yet? Why don't I show you around?'

Wordlessly Lily nodded, getting to her feet, almost hypnotised, starting slightly as he took her hand and led her away from the party. Appetising barbecue smells wafted over and Lily could see children dancing, young people eying each other up and friends joking and talking. The sun was setting and the fairy lights took on an otherworldly gleam in the dusk as they walked, still hand in hand, towards the path that led back to the villa.

Casually, slowly Damir began to draw small circles on the back of her hand as he held it. Languorous, light, almost casual touches that burned through her, sending licks of fire shooting up her arm and spreading throughout her body.

'I thought you were showing me around, I already know this way,' she said, and he laughed, low and deep and rumbling, vibrating deliciously through her.

'Trust me.'

His words hung in the air, then Lily nodded, her clasp tightening on his as Damir led her to the top of the steep path that bisected the narrow island. Instead of continuing straight on to Fire Cove and the villa, he turned left, leading her up a narrow, twisting path that climbed higher and higher through the trees until, after a couple of minutes, they emerged onto the hill-top, Lokvar spread out before them.

On one side the sun hung low over Fire Cove, on the other they could see and hear the lights and the sounds from the party. Before them lay the headland dominated by Damir's hotel, behind them the island tapered to a point, the end marked by the old medieval monastery, now just pictur-esque ruins. Beyond that was the main-land, barely visible in the rapidly darkening dusk.

'I used to come here when I was a boy,' he said. 'To look out at all this and swear...'

'Swear what?'

'That one day this would all be mine.'

'And is it?'

'Almost.'

'Quite the conqueror.'

'I try.'

'Oh, I bet you do. And I bet you succeed. Who could resist?'

Her words were teasing, but as she spoke the atmosphere became charged. Lily was so close, her hand still lay in his, her touch light yet searing through him. He could feel the slight movement as she breathed, smell the lemon of her shampoo, the sharp floral scent of her perfume and all thought of business disappeared, something more primal replacing it. She was warm, she was real and she was, oh, so desirable. He turned to look at her, at the sheet of golden hair falling down her back, her curves displayed by the silk vest top, at her long-lashed eyes, and he couldn't resist the urge to reach out and touch her cheek, one finger straying to caress the curve of her mouth.

Lily jolted, a small almost imperceptible move before she stilled under his touch. She wanted him, he knew it in every fibre. Despite their brief acquaintance, attraction burned between them, so tangible he could almost hear it sizzle. But this relationship wasn't about attraction, the stakes were far higher and wooing her was only supposed to go so far. Damir knew that the sensible thing to do would be to make a joke, lighten the atmosphere and head back to the party. He wanted Lily onside but that didn't mean seducing her. However, for once business wasn't the first thing on his mind. For once his need filled him, the air almost palpable with want.

And then all thought fled as Lily's hand tightened on his and she moved a little closer, turning a little more until she faced him fully, tilting her face to his, eyes half-closed as Damir traced the sweet lines of her face, his fingertips trailing down her cheek, the curve of her chin and down her long neck, lingering at the sweet spot where her pulse beat wildly, before moving onto her bare shoulder and coming to rest on her back. She swallowed, biting her lip as she looked at him, blue eyes full of shifting emotions. Damir paused, one hand splayed on her back, the other white-knuckled as he waited for permission or refusal.

'Is this part of the tour?' Her voice was a little hoarse, husking out the words as if her throat was full.

He smiled then, slow and full of intent. 'Not usually.'

Her eyes darkened to navy. 'But this evening?'

Damir didn't answer, he just stared at Lily steadily and she looked back, the questions and confusion ebbing away as she moved her hand up his arm, trailing it lightly over his skin until she reached his shoulder, further up until it was her turn to explore his face, each light touch like liquid flame. Sensation pulsed through him, hot and sweet and almost painful as she teased her way down his cheek, her fingers tracing the lines of his mouth, the sensitive skin behind his ears, her face intent as if she was learning him by heart.

'Lily?' It was both question and entreaty, begging her for permission, and she nodded, face solemn, lips half-parted in anticipation.

Primal need filled him. Damir wanted nothing more than to rush, to crush her to him, to explore her mouth, her body, to hear her moan and sigh and call his name, to tumble her onto the ground and cover her with his body. He wanted to tear at their clothes, for there to be no barriers between them. And he could do it, he knew it, sensed it as the air around them danced with the haze of desire; she wanted him as much as he wanted her. But he held himself back.

Slowly, every movement full of intent, he pulled her to him, one hand still on her back, the other clasping the curve of her waist. She was tall but still a head shorter than him and he had to dip his head to taste her. It was a light kiss, an exploratory kiss, an anticipatory promise of what could be, and it overwhelmed him like no kiss had for longer than he cared to remember. She tasted of salt, of sweetness, like sunshine and the sea, and he wanted to sink into her and never surface.

Lily made a small sound like a whimper as she stepped closer, crushing the curves of her body against him, and Damir groaned as he felt the softness of her breasts against his chest, her long legs tangling with his. 'Lily,' he said, this time in wonder, and she smiled against his mouth as she kissed him back. This second kiss was deeper, her mouth opening to his as she ran her hands along the planes of his back, setting him alight with every touch.

Still he held back, not allowing the flames to burn them, managing with a Herculean effort to not pick her up and lay her on the ground. They had all night, they could even have all summer, and anticipation would only make the coming together sweeter. But it still took all he had not to rush her, to allow her to set the pace.

Damir had no idea how long they stood there. The kiss deepened and intensified until he was consumed by her, every part of him aching to explore every part of her. He dragged his mouth from hers, ignoring her moan of protest, as he tasted her throat, her shoulder, as his fingers edged up her body, under her top, caressing every rib until he reached the underside of her breast, skin giving way to the lace of her bra.

Impatient, he slipped his thumb underneath the material, needing the warmth of flesh, and heard her gasp as his hand slid up to cup her, as she leaned into his touch. His need for her was evident, palpable, almost painful but still he stood, taking his time, letting her take hers, giving her every opportunity to walk away.

But she didn't walk away. Instead she pressed even closer so it was his turn to moan, the friction of her body against his torture. 'Lily,' he managed on a ragged breath. For a moment he didn't think she'd heard him as her mouth found his shoulder, and then she stood back. He was instantly cold, wanting to do nothing but to crush her against him, but he restrained himself, overwhelmed by how fast they'd ignited. It was nothing like the seductive games he was used to and the realisation of how close he'd veered to losing control scared him.

'I…' Her breath was as out of time as his, her chest heaving, pupils dilated, eyelids heavy. 'I guess I'm not as bad at flirting as I thought I was.'

He half closed his eyes, torn between a groan and a laugh. 'Oh, you're not bad at all.'

Was that all this was? Flirting? He needed to process what had happened, to figure out how his emotions, his body had escaped his usual iron-clad control. To figure out what happened next because that kind of desire, that kind of want was incompatible with the man he needed to be. The man he had to be. The man he was.

'Are you still up for showing me around some more?'

'If you want me to.'

'I'm only here for a short while. It would be a shame not to see a little bit more.' Her meaning was implicit. She had one summer. One summer for him to convince her that he was the best custodian for Fire Cove. Damir knew that mixing business with pleasure was a mistake but he also knew that it would be very hard to pull back now.

'It would,' he agreed. 'There's a lot to see and do. I'd hate for you miss out.'

'Great. I'm looking forward to the next part of the tour.' She looked around and shivered. 'It's getting dark.'

'We should head back.' To other people, the safety in numbers, to give his body time to recover and his mind the opportunity to regain control. Damir extracted his phone and handed it to her. 'Give me your number and I'll arrange a date. You don't get seasick, do you?'

'Not as far as I know.' She quickly pressed a few keys and handed it back. 'Damir…' She paused then took a deep breath. 'Look, I have never been the sneak out of parties to make out with a guy kind of girl, I was usually the hang out in a kitchen and then leave early to study type. But, like I said, I want this summer to be different. So thank you, for making me feel so welcome. For offering to show me around. I really appreciate it.'

'Really, there is no need to thank me, I'm enjoying getting to know you,' Damir said smoothly as he started to make his way down the path, realising that in just a few minutes it would be totally dark. He felt curiously flat. He should be congratulating himself on the perfect start to his campaign to get Lily onside—but instead for the first time in a long time he was conscious of doubt. Getting his hands on the villa was as important as ever. But was he really willing to deceive Lily to do it? Or, judging by his out-of-control response, was it really himself he was deceiving?

CHAPTER FIVE

IT WAS THE perfect day for a boat ride. Almost too perfect, the sun out in force, the sea flat enough to please all but the most sensitive sailor. The omens were good for the day ahead. A day in which Damir was going to stick to the plan: give Lily an unforgettable day but stay in control of both his reactions and the situation.

It all sounded so easy when he put it like that.

Damir checked his arrangements one last time, preparation being key to a successful campaign. All was in order with freshly laundered cushions and blankets heaped on the cabin seat and a delicious selection of food, wine and beer chilling in the fridge. Everything was perfect.

He just needed Lily to actually show up.

'Hi, sorry I'm late.' Lily panted up to the

boat, a bag slung casually over her shoulder, hair scooped back into a loose ponytail. She looked ethereal in a blue sundress that floated down to mid-ankle, teamed with flat silver sandals, and Damir's stomach tightened in automatic reaction to her presence.

'Not at all,' he said, extending a hand to take her surprisingly heavy bag before helping her into the boat, conscious of the feel of her hand in his. He hadn't seen her in the few days since the party. He'd thought the time apart sufficient to assert sense over emotions. It was possible he'd miscalculated as electricity zipped up his arm when she took his hand. 'I know it's an early start, but it gets very busy in the old town later on.'

'I don't mind early starts, at home I'm usually in the office around seven-thirty. Thank you.' She let go of his hand and looked around. 'Oh, this is beautiful! I didn't realise when you said boat ride that you meant anything this fancy. I would have done my hair and worn more make-up if I'd known. I'm going to let the boat down.'

'You look fine.' She looked a lot more

than fine, honey-coloured hair falling around her face, her skin very lightly tanned, set off by the thin straps of the dress. Long and loose, the light fabric swirled around her body, showing off more of her curves than it hid. Damir realised that he was staring and with difficulty pulled his attention back to the conversation. 'The boat is mine. Glad you like her.' He tried for nonchalant, but couldn't hide his pride.

Like all island children Damir had been taught to sail before he could walk, but this boat was nothing like the small sailboats he'd grown up with. Teak and chrome, low in the water and speedy, it exuded class—and discreetly said money.

The deck included a large sunbathing platform and a table flanked by two padded benches, perfect for sunset drinks and intimate dinners. Below deck was a small sitting room and kitchenette, a shower room and a separate bedroom, just large enough to fit a small double bed. Despite its compact size the boat was fitted out to the highest specs and worthy of Lily's evident admiration.

'I don't just like it, I think I'm in love,' she said. 'Can I have a tour?'

'Of course.' He didn't need to be asked twice, showing off every cubbyhole, every beautifully carved finish, talking through the engine specifications in detail, until her responses became a little more formulaic, her expression more polite than enthused.

'Apologies,' he said, a little ruefully. 'My enthusiasm tends to run away with me where this beauty is concerned.'

Lily ran one caressing hand over the glossy teak finish and Damir watched her trailing fingers, envying his own boat. 'No, no, that's quite okay. Far be it from me to get between a man and his great passion.'

'It's true,' he admitted. 'There will always be three in any relationship I have.'

'At least you're up front about it. And I'm sure your girlfriends don't mind sharing you with someone so special.'

'I haven't had any trouble so far,' he told her teasingly. 'What do you think? Would you mind sharing?'

'Luckily I'm not the jealous type.' Colour edged her cheekbones as she spoke and she twisted round to look out to sea.

The memory of the passionate kiss they'd shared hung in the air and Damir quickly changed the subject. Control was the theme of the day, and that kiss had been anything but.

'I hope you don't get seasick because I'm planning to take the scenic route today. It only takes forty-five minutes to sail into the City Port, but it's a taxi ride to the old city from there or a fairly hilly half-hour walk. So I'm planning to sail a longer route, past Sunset Bay and into the old harbour. We'll go right past the city walls so you can see them in all their glory from the sea—and get some understanding why Dubrovnik was so good at withstanding sieges. And why it's the go-to destination for historical film crews as well.'

'That all sounds amazing,' Lily said. 'Longer sail, view of the walls, all of it. Thank you for taking the time to do this for me. Is there anything I can do to help?'

'Have you ever been on a boat like this before?'

'Not as much as a dinghy. But I'm a quick learner.'

'In that case, get ready to catch this rope.

You can coil it up and then hang it on that hook there. Ready?'

Damir issued a few quick instructions as he prepared to cast off and Lily was quick to catch his meaning, surefooted and steady as she helped him push the boat away from the mooring post. She stood next to him as he started the engine and began to guide the small boat away from the island, asking questions about what he was doing and why, seemingly genuinely interested in his answers.

Damir, normally possessive of his boat, insisted she take the wheel once they were clear of Lokvar and their course set, guiding and coaching her as she gingerly increased speed in order to drive the boat at a steady pace across the calm, blue sea.

'You've got a knack for this, good job,' he said as he took the tiller back and she grinned with unfeigned joy.

'Even I couldn't mess up on a straight line with no other boats within one hundred yards either side. I don't think I'd be comfortable gliding into the harbour and stopping alongside the platform the way you do. And I certainly don't think I could

manage if there were any waves at all. Oh!'
She scooped up her bag and held it up tri-
umphantly.

'I forgot! I made some cakes last night.
You wouldn't believe the way Antun
watched me every second I was in the
kitchen. He evidently did *not* trust me not
to set something on fire or mess up his
precious oven. But they came out okay
and Ana gave me some of those amazing
spinach pastries she makes as well. Don't
tell anybody, but I also managed to snaffle
some of that gorgeous home-made lemonade Antun makes. I don't know what his
recipe is, he guards it with his life. I could
get us some lemonade now. Do you have
any cups or anything?'

'Look in the gallery. You'll find ice and
glasses there.'

'Great, I'll be as quick as I can.'

And she was gone, bag over her shoulder, humming as she navigated the narrow ladder. Damir concentrated on the
distant horizon, processing the conversation. He had invited a reasonable number
of women out for a day—or an evening—
sail over the last couple of years. They'd all

arrived dressed in expensive teeny bikinis and luxurious wraps, expecting him to provide champagne and delicious, dainty food as a matter of course. Not one had baked before the trip, or had thought to pick up something to bring.

The unwritten assumption was that as the host, and a host who was known to be wealthy, he would treat them to the entire trip. And that was fine, he shared those expectations, knew what was required, and it had never been an issue. He just hadn't realised how good it would feel to have someone think about treating him as well.

Lily peered up eagerly as the boat finally rounded the curve of the coastline and the imposing walls finally came into sight.

'Oh! Oh, Damir!' She wasn't sure she could open her eyes any wider as she drank in the view, taking off her sunglasses so as not to miss a detail, even though the sun already reflected brightly off the water, the light bouncing dazzlingly off the old walls. 'It's magnificent. I've seen pictures, of course, and heard stories, many stories, but nothing could have prepared me for this. I can't believe you're lucky enough to live here.'

Neither could she believe that Josip had never returned here. If Dubrovnik had been her home city, nothing would keep her away, certainly not for years and years on end. If there was anything the last few months had taught her it was how important moving forward was, learning from the past and not being haunted by it. Maybe that was a lesson she should try and pass on to her stepfather as well.

This time Lily didn't offer to help as Damir deftly steered the boat into the already crowded old harbour, securing a mooring spot with a satisfied grin. She could barely contain her impatience as he securely fastened the boat before lightly jumping onto the wooden walkway and helping her out.

'This is why I told you to be ready so early,' he said, leading her towards the arched entrance into the fabled old city. 'As you can see, it's already pretty busy, but in less than an hour the cruise ship passengers will arrive and this street will be jostling room only. If you want to walk the walls, and I assume you do, then getting here as early as possible is essential.'

'I absolutely do want to walk the walls. In fact, I don't want to leave any tourist trap untouched. You are allowed to be my tour guide, but you can't be a local, dismissive of anything that's popular. I want to do all the tacky touristy bits. I'm going to consider it research, because otherwise I'll feel like a fool when I'm talking to the guests and they know more about Dubrovnik than I do.'

'Your wish is my command.' He smiled at her, sweet and slow, and Lily was conscious of her heart squeezing as he did so.

Don't get carried away, she told herself. Apart from helping her onto and off the boat, Damir had made no move to touch her, hadn't flirted with her, all morning, just as the texts they had exchanged to set this day up had been merely friendly, not flirtatious. It was almost as if the kiss just a few nights ago had never been.

But there was an acute consciousness between them, an awareness of each other's every move, a carefulness in their conversation that showed the kiss was very much on both of their minds. Whether that meant a repetition or not she didn't know. Part of her hoped so, wanted to allow the attraction to run its course, but she was also scared by the fierceness of her reaction to him. If Damir hadn't stopped, would they have ended up making love on the ground? Up against a tree? She couldn't say, hand on heart, that it was an impossibility.

Neither could she honestly say that she hadn't spent more than one idle moment wondering just what that lovemaking might have felt like…

She wrenched her mind back to the present as Damir guided her through the marble streets, Lily slowing to marvel at enticing alleyways running off on every side. Some were dead ends, others led to picturesque squares or to long, steep stone steps. But every time she slowed, Damir hustled her on, giving her no time to stop, stare, take pictures or set foot in any of the shops or restaurants. Instead, Damir marched her on until they'd secured tickets and ascended the stairs that led them to the top of the famous city walls.

Lily knew that in the heat of midday,

once the city was full of day trippers, cruise ship passengers and tourists pouring in from the hotels from all around Dubrovnik, it could be shuffling room only on the walls. Early as it was, there were still plenty of people walking along the wide turreted walkways, looking down on the one side into courtyards, windows and alleyways and on the other across the blue, blue sea. But there was plenty of room for everyone, and now Lily could stop as much she wanted, and take as many photos she wished, playfully pulling Damir in for a couple of selfies despite his protestations.

It was a surprisingly long way round, with some unexpectedly steep climbs as the sun grew hotter and hotter and the walls busier and busier. Lily wished she could take a slower walk round in the cool of an early spring or autumnal day, one when the tourists were few and the sun less intense. But despite the heat and hubbub, it was still one of the most awe-inspiring experiences of her life and when they finally descended, Lily's head was spinning with the history and the tales Damir had told her, her eyes and heart full of all she'd seen.

It seemed impossible that the old town itself could compare with its own defensive walls, but a place where the roads were literally made of marble, and every house was hundreds of years old, couldn't help but intrigue her and she explored every alley, stopping only for an ice cream and some much-needed water.

'Okay,' Damir said after a while. 'We've been walking for hours and I for one am ready for a beer. Luckily I know the perfect place.'

'A beer?' Lily wasn't much of a beer drinker, happy with the odd glass of wine now and then. Her mother's struggles with alcohol and drugs had left Lily cautious about overindulging and daytime drinking really wasn't her thing.

'Or a soft drink of your choice, but the place I'm taking you to deserves to be toasted with a real libation.'

Intrigued, Lily accompanied Damir through yet another bewildering route of alleyways, small open squares and stairs. She should have brought breadcrumbs with her to scatter or a ball of thread as left to herself she would never find her way out again, but Damir was sure and certain of his route.

Finally they came to a small archway. A chalkboard by the archway simply said '*Bar*' with an arrow pointing through. Damir indicated that Lily should go first and, intrigued, she walked through, eyes widening in awe as she took in the scene before her.

The bar was perched on rocks that seemed to tumble down to the sea far below, tables positioned by railings that were all that stood between the bar's patrons and the rocks below. The rocks formed a kind of natural terrace, the bar on the top and tables on several levels beneath, each joined by a flat stone staircase. The fourth level was the largest and had no tables. On it a small group of young men congregated, talking noisily, all wearing just their swimming shorts.

As Lily watched one of them stepped up to the very edge and with no fanfare executed a perfect dive far down into the sea below. She gasped as she watched him go, his bronzed body momentarily gleaming in the sunlight before it fell. 'Fancy a swim?' Damir said with a grin.

'You must be kidding, there's no way I'm jumping off there.' Lily eyed the steep drop and shivered.

'That's one way into the water, but alternatively you could just climb down there.' And Damir pointed to a narrow ladder leading from the diving rock to a cluster of rocks just above sea level. A few groups were sunbathing on towels spread out over the hard surface, others had climbed into the water and were swimming out. This was no shallow, safe cove or cordoned-off area with land on both sides, these swimmers headed straight into the depths of the Adriatic, sharing the water with boats and kayaks. It looked exhilarating.

'You have your costume?' Damir asked, and she nodded.

'Yes, you told me to make sure I wore it.' Lily followed Damir carefully climbing down the steep ladder until she reached the rocks below. Unselfconsciously, Damir shed his clothes, standing there in just his trunks. Lily's gaze wandered appreciatively over his wide torso, narrow waist and strong legs, lust shooting through her with unexpected possessiveness.

'Come on,' he said with a boyish grin. 'What are you waiting for?'

Nobody was paying them any attention as Lily slipped off her long dress and her sandals. In her bag she had a pair of sea shoes, having been warned about the dangers of sea urchins on Croatia's rocky coast. She noticed that no local seem to wear them and Damir raised an eyebrow as she slightly defiantly slipped them on but she was glad of their protection as they walked over the rough rock until they reached one of the ubiquitous ladders that led into the Adriatic depths. Lily didn't allow herself time to stop and think about the cold. As soon as she was deep enough in she let go, straight into the bracing water, swimming fast until her limbs warmed up.

She didn't know how long they spent out there but she could have stayed there for ever, turning into a water nymph who lived in these turquoise waters. Bobbing in the water, she looked up at the walls rising far above her and felt a kinship with all the hundreds of generations of people who must've swum in this very spot.

They swam for at least half an hour, reluctantly returning to dry off on the rocks like a pair of mer-people, letting the sun dry them until they could put their clothes back over their swimsuits. Then, glowing with the warmth and the exercise, they clambered back up the ladder to the bar, where Damir procured a table right on the rocky outcrop, presenting Lily with a beer that she decided she did want after all. 'This place is amazing,' she said as she took an appreciative gulp of the bitter, amber liquid.

'It's a Dubrovnik institution,' Damir told her. 'It's one of those places that is in all the guidebooks, that everybody who has been here tells their friends is a must-visit and yet it always feels unspoilt, like you're the first person to have discovered it. Even at the height of the season, when it's at peak busyness, it feels as if there's space for everyone who needs to be here.'

'You come here a lot then?' Of course, she remembered, Damir didn't live on Lokvar but somewhere here in Dubrovnik.

'I haven't been here in over seven years.' His sunglasses hid his expression, but his voice was carefully emotionless.

'Oh?' Lily tried to match his lack of emotion, not wanting to show how curious she was.

'It's a favourite spot of my ex-wife's. We used to come here a lot. After she left, I found new places to go, ones without so many memories.'

And yet he had brought her here. Lily didn't know how to interpret that, but her stomach tumbled as she tried not to show her surprise—or how flattered she was.

'I'm sorry that your marriage didn't work out.' Seven years ago? He could only have been in his mid-twenties when they'd divorced.

He shrugged. 'It happens. In the end we wanted different things.'

'Such as?'

'Kata wanted a normal life. A family, a husband who was home for dinner with weekends off. She resented how much time I spent working. Meanwhile my father wanted to expand the business, needed me to step up, evenings, weekends, whatever it took. After he died the pressure intensified. We just stopped communicating and she left. She's remarried now, has a child.' He paused. 'I think she's happy.'

'I'm sorry,' she said softly, covering his hand with hers. 'For your father, your marriage, all of it.'

'We got together when we were at school, maybe we were too young when we married. Too busy living in the present to prepare for the future. How about you?' He turned his hand to clasp hers, his fingers folding around her palm, and Lily suddenly found it hard to concentrate, all of her being focussed on the sensations pulsing through her hand, zipping through her entire body.

'Me?' She managed to somehow answer his question. 'No, I've never been married. I've never even lived with a partner. Career first, my love life a very poor second.'

'It's hard to balance the two.'

'It is. Date someone with the same ethos and you run the risk of never seeing them, date someone with different priorities and they soon get bored with your limited availability. I was with this one guy, a lawyer in my firm, for a couple of years but when we broke up last year it didn't make any real difference to my life. I missed the convenience of him rather than Seb himself, and I'm sure he felt the same way.'

Lily looked straight ahead out at the almost overwhelming brightness of the sea and sighed. 'I look at my mum and Josip and they are so easy with each other, they really are two halves of the same whole, cheesy as that sounds. I've never felt like that about anybody. But then I haven't wanted to either, not while I was working towards being partner. It would be too distracting, having to factor in someone else's life and needs.'

Although that's not how her mum and Josip seemed. They just supported each other through all life's ups and downs, including her mother's decision to finally get a university degree and a career in her thirties. Sometimes Lily envied them, but she had no idea how to let someone get that close. How to be that vulnerable. The only person who she'd allowed in was Izzy— and now she was more alone than ever.

'That's it.' Damir nodded. 'You get it, to

build something like a career or a business you have to be single-minded. And finding someone who understands, who isn't resentful of that is hard.'

'So you've been single since you divorced?' That didn't fit with Ana's playboy assessment, or with the easy charm he displayed with her.

'Single? No. But I'm not looking for anything serious and I am very clear about that. I don't want to break any hearts or raise any expectations. But if I like someone and they like me, and we want to spend some time together then great.' His hand tightened on hers and Lily's breath quickened. 'For instance, I like you, Lily, and I think you like me. I would very much enjoy getting to know you better while you're in Croatia.'

'Get to know me better? Is that code for a few trips out like this or for a no-strings, one-summer-only kind of deal?' She managed to sound nonchalant, as though she was always being propositioned by gorgeous, sun-bronzed men in idyllic locations, although her throat was thick, her ears buzzing and her pulse pounded.

'No code, simply getting to know each other better and seeing where it leads. If it leads nowhere, fine, otherwise we part when one of us has had enough or at the end of the summer with no hard feelings and some good memories. What do you think?'

What did she think? Lily was already overwhelmed by her physical reaction to Damir. She might not have put a lot of effort into her love life before, but she had also never had a fling. She was more of a few polite dates, gradually working up to formal couple status kind of girl. Was she emotionally able to cope with the kind of short-term relationship Damir was offering?

But she was supposed to be living spontaneously and trying new things, to be less sensible and have more fun. And she suspected she would have a lot of fun if she said yes.

She picked up her beer, willing her hand to steady, not to show any sign of nerves, and held her bottle up to his. 'I think we should drink to getting to know each other better. To the summer.'

'To the summer,' he echoed, his dark eyes opaque. 'I am very much looking forward to seeing how this turns out.'

'Me too.' And to her surprise Lily meant it. She wasn't going to plan or organise and schedule. She was going to wait and see and enjoy every moment of this unexpected summer romance.

CHAPTER SIX

'ARE YOU SURE you don't mind, Lily? You haven't had a day off for a week, and now you're cancelling your plans.' Ana looked worriedly at Lily, who gave the older woman a determined smile.

'Of course I don't mind. I can meet Damir any time.'

'But you have restaurant reservations—I heard there's a waiting list to get in there.'

'Well, Damir only suggested it a couple of days ago, so either he has a standing reservation or he can pull some strings. Either way, if I don't go it's not the end of the world. I'd be more than happy to go back to the seafood burger takeaway in the old town we visited last week. I've never eaten anything more delicious and I can do that any time.'

'But you've worked so hard. You deserve a break.'

'I'm fine, honestly. Ivona is no use to anyone until that swelling goes down. She's in a lot of pain. As are you, so go and lie down and stop worrying about me.'

Lily shooed Ana up the stairs, not allowing her smile to slip until the older woman was out of sight and then she leaned against the wall and let out a deep sigh. She would never have confessed it to Ana, but truthfully she was more than a little disappointed to cancel her much-anticipated afternoon and evening off. Damir been called away to a meeting in Zagreb earlier in the week, which meant she hadn't seen him since he'd sailed her back to Lokvar after their day out in Dubrovnik, receiving just a few texts in the week since.

What was the point of throwing a lifetime of caution to the wind and agreeing to a summer fling if you were both too busy to *do* any actual flinging?

Today was supposed to change all that. She had the afternoon and evening off and Damir, who was due to arrive back from Zagreb this morning, had offered to pick her up in the early afternoon and show her more of the coastline from his boat, before finishing the day off with a meal at an exclusive restaurant in Dubrovnik. The kind of restaurant Lily needed to dress up for. A real date restaurant.

But not today. Thanks to Ivona's sprained ankle and Ana's migraine they were two members of staff down. Lily had to step in. With a second heartfelt sigh, Lily pulled her phone out of her shorts pocket and quickly composed an apology to Damir. She stared at the message for a few minutes before pressing 'Send'. It was done. Hopefully he would be as understanding about her schedule as she had been about his—and if not, then, casual or not, this fledgling relationship was never going to take off.

Ignoring the disappointment that lay heavy on her chest, Lily tilted her chin and marched out to the beach café where she was needed to serve drinks and take payment for beach chairs.

Every table in the café-bar, every sun lounger was occupied. Lily couldn't believe the difference a couple of weeks made.

Dubrovnik itself was busy all year round, a popular city break no matter what the weather, and the Dalmatian Riviera also enjoyed an extended season from late spring right the way through to Halloween, when the bustling resorts wound down for the winter break. Lokvar, however, like many of Croatia's many islands, enjoyed a much shorter season. But it made up for length with intensity. The B&B was fully booked for the weeks and months ahead, and every morning day trippers arrived early to enjoy Fire Cove and kept on coming throughout the day and into the evening—all happy to order drinks and food from the beach café. Unassuming as the café was, Marija was sitting on quite a little gold mine.

The rest of the morning and lunchtime passed quickly as Lily took orders and delivered drinks and snacks, keeping an eye on the sunbeds and beach chairs to make sure each occupant had paid for using them. Exhausting though it was, she found she enjoyed the constant buzz and dealing with such a variety of people from all over the world. Contract law was often solitary, just her, her computer and hundreds of lines of text to scrutinise. She'd thought she preferred life that way but maybe she'd been wrong.

Smiling at a happy, sand-covered family, Lily collected the empty plates and glasses from their table and began to manoeuvre her way back through to the kitchen, when she caught a glimpse of a figure waiting by the framed menu at the café entrance.

'I'll be with you in a minute,' she called over her shoulder, relieved that so far the vast majority of her customers spoke English no matter what their nationality and determined to spend some time with her language app that evening.

'Take your time,' the figure said in familiar tones, and Lily stopped stock still, almost dropping the heaped tray as she did so.

'Damir? Didn't you get my message? I am so sorry but I have had to cancel our plans. We're short-staffed and I'm needed here.'

'I know.' He sauntered towards her, quirking an eyebrow at the tray. 'Do you need a hand with that?' Before she could protest he took it from her.

'Thank you. But if you know I can't make it then why are you here?'

'We have a date.'

'Yes, but…'

'Maybe not the date we originally planned, but I thought we could improvise. What do you need me to do?'

'What do I…?' Lily blinked. Had she heard him correctly? 'What do you mean?'

'You said you were two people down? Luckily I was working in a café from the time I was old enough to collect glasses.' He held up the tray, effortlessly balanced in one hand. 'So put me to work.'

'I can't ask you to do that, you've been in meetings all week…' But she was torn. Luka was behind the bar, which meant she was covering both the café and the beach. Easy enough when it was quiet, almost impossible when it was as busy as this. Besides, she had been looking forward to spending time with Damir.

'You haven't asked, I offered. Lily, I've been in meetings all week and the only thing that kept me going was the thought of seeing you today. So if this is what I have to do…'

He didn't look like someone who had been in meetings all week and who had flown across the country this morning, he looked almost piratical with his dark wind-swept hair, the graze of stubble outlining his jaw and rolled-up white sleeves show-casing strong capable wrists. 'Can you mix drinks? Make coffee?' she asked hopefully.

'Of course.'

'Because then Luka can manage the beach and I can stick to waitressing in here. You really don't mind giving up your Saturday afternoon?'

'I want to spend my Saturday afternoon with you,' he said, the heat in his gaze causing the rest of the busy café to fade away as she stood there, unable to move, unsure what to say.

'I don't know how to thank you,' she managed at last, and he winked.

'I'm sure I'll think of something suitable.'

'Two small beers, one large, a Shirley Temple, a lemonade and an Irish coffee,' Lily panted as she passed Damir the order note, scooping up the tray of coffees he'd just brewed with a quick smile. Her cheeks were flushed with the heat and exercise as she rushed around the terrace, her hair pulled back into a jaunty ponytail. She wore practical black shorts and a white T-shirt teamed with a small apron—not at all how he'd envisioned her looking when he picked her up for their date. Yet all he wanted to do was pull her into a corner and kiss her until they were both gasping for air.

'On it,' Damir promised, as he lined the glasses up before him, mentally running through the ingredients for a Shirley Temple. To his surprise he was enjoying the fast pace, even though spending his precious time making endless coffees, pouring endless beers and concocting endless sickly-sweet cocktails was not how Damir had planned to spend this afternoon. What he had planned was the next phase in the wooing Lily campaign after an unexpectedly excellent start.

He hadn't intended to mix business with pleasure quite as thoroughly as things had turned out, but the more he thought about it—and there were times when he could think about little else—the more sense it made. He was genuinely attracted to Lily and she was attracted to him. Why deny themselves an enjoyable few weeks or months just because he needed something from her?

And that was all this was. A few enjoyable weeks. So he had decided to come and help her out? It wasn't that uncharacteristic.

Only of course it was. Damir couldn't remember the last time he'd put himself out for another person, the last time he'd stood behind a bar rather than sat behind a desk, the last time he'd received orders rather than given them, but to his surprise the afternoon faded into evening long before he got bored.

'Okay, bartender, your shift is over.'

He looked up from the mojito he was garnishing to see Lily leaning on the bar, her hair now down and grazing her shoulders, her apron tossed over her arm.

'The night shift is here. It's time to collect your wages,' she said.

'Wages?'

'Payment in kind,' she amended. 'Dinner and whatever you want to drink. Antun is making us pizzas as I speak so get yourself a drink and come and sit down. You deserve it.'

The last ferry had departed and the café died down to a pleasant hum of regulars, those staying on the island and those with their own boats or charters, so they managed to grab a table at the end of the terrace, looking over Fire Cove. At this time of day it was easy to see where the bay had got its name from, the sun lying heavy and low, casting a golden path on the darkening sea, the sky a hundred different shades of red, orange and pink.

'It is so beautiful,' Lily said with a sigh. 'Every day I think that has to be the most beautiful sunset yet, and then the next day tops it. I can't believe I'm lucky enough to be here.'

'It's a gorgeous spot,' he agreed. 'So much potential.'

He hesitated, wondering whether to say more when Antun emerged from his kitchen in person to place pizza and salad on the table and for the next couple of minutes they were busy helping themselves to slices of hot, heaped pizza, forking the fresh salad onto their plates.

'Mmm, this is delicious,' Lily mumbled. 'I'm sure the place you had in mind was amazing too, but I'm not sure anything can beat this view and freshly made pizza with Antun's secret tomato sauce recipe.' She took a sip of her wine. 'What did you mean just now when you said potential?'

This was it. This was his moment. Damir did his best to sound nonchalant, as though he hadn't thought about nothing but this topic for years. 'Only that this is the best spot not just on Lokvar but possibly on the whole of the coast. The water is safe, the beach perfect, the view as you said is spectacular, and yet only a handful of people get to stay here. Don't you think it would be the perfect setting for a hotel complex? Rooms, sports facilities, a beach club, a five-star restaurant with floor-to-ceiling windows? I always think it's a shame that the tourist season is so short on Lokvar, especially when so many livelihoods depend on it. A resort here could change all that.' He sat back and picked up his beer bottle, every sense attuned to her reaction.

Lily looked around as if envisioning what he'd described. 'I can see what you mean, this place is blessed with everything and I guess the beach bar and villa are pretty basic, but don't you think that's part of the charm? I love how it's so democratic, anyone can come here for a swim or picnic, or rent a chair for just a few *kuna*, whether they're backpackers or own their own yachts. Besides, the villa has been in Marija's family for generations. I can't imagine her selling it and I don't see her wanting to do that kind of development at her age—or at all to be honest.'

'So will Josip come back one day, do you think?'

Her expression clouded. 'No, I don't think so. I don't know what will happen. Whether Ana will take over running it or Marija will sell it. To be honest, I think she's refusing to make plans, hoping Josip will change his mind.'

'And he won't?'

She shook her head slowly. 'I don't see it. He doesn't even talk about Lokvar much, but he must think about it all the time. How could you not miss this with all your soul? Don't you? I get it's more exciting in Dubrovnik, and it's beautiful there too, but there is something so special about Lokvar.'

'It's not really practical for me to live here. Once my father expanded onto the mainland we all moved. I do have a house here, but I don't use it. After Kata left I just wasn't here enough to justify running it so I converted it into a holiday let instead.'

Lily's eyes narrowed and she sat back. 'That reminds me, you weren't entirely honest with me the first time we met.'

'Oh?' Guilt, unexpected and unwelcome, twisted through his chest. It was so easy to forget his subterfuge while sitting out under the darkening sky. Every time he was with Lily, despite his vows to maintain the necessary emotional distance.

'A café, you said, a few apartments on the mainland. You didn't mention the hotel here, or the hotels and restaurants all around Dubrovnik. You practically own the whole island according to Ana.'

That lack of honesty. 'I didn't want to impress you for the wrong reasons. My grandfather had ambitions and started to fulfil them, my father carried them on and I have taken what they started and been very successful. I'm proud of that, but I don't want to be judged on it, especially by pretty strangers. I wanted to take you out because you liked me, not because you liked my portfolio.'

'I wouldn't have said yes because of what you have, it's who a person is that interests me.' She took another bite of pizza. 'So was it your dream as well to be a hotel tycoon or were you indoctrinated from a young age?'

A dream of his own? He'd never really allowed himself to consider such a thing. It was easier not to think about what could have been when what must be was so clear. 'I'm the only son of an only son. The Kozina ambition was pretty much instilled in me from birth. I told you I was collecting glasses as soon as I could carry them. By the time I was twenty there wasn't a job in the café or hotel I hadn't done, including working on the building crew. I studied business at university but my apprenticeship was here. With my grandfather and father.' Now he was the only one left. His failure to remarry, to father sons to carry on the business lay heavy on him. He knew his duty.

'But what if it hadn't been your family's dream? Take me, I knew I wanted to be a lawyer from a young age. Not because I had a passion for sub-clauses but because I knew it was a career that signified stability and success, respect. And that seemed enough. But since I came to Lokvar I've wondered who I might have been if I hadn't yearned for that stability. If I'd followed my heart.' She laughed, twisting the stem of her wine glass in her hands. 'Not that I have any answer to that yet. But I chose that, you didn't have a choice by the sound of it. Is there a part of you that wishes he'd been, oh, I don't know, a musician or an accountant or a teacher? Anything?'

'The only possible other profession my family would have been happy with is a professional footballer and I am nowhere near good enough. Lily, it's not as simple as wishes and wants. Around here, tourism pays the bills of nearly everyone, it has for a long time. And it's better to be the ones controlling that, profiting from it, than the ones losing out to it. This coastline has a long, bloody and difficult history, conquered over and over, annexed to too many empires.

'To be here, free, successful, respected? It's a luxury my ancestors could never have dreamed of. Even my father lived through a period of turmoil. Of uncertainty. He saw his country fall apart, saw war and devastation and hatred. No wonder he came out of that wanting control of his destiny, to own his land, to ensure our roots were so firmly planted we could never be torn out. He worked tirelessly, constantly to make that happen. I am honoured to carry on his dream.'

He looked out over the now-dark sea. His father's untimely death, the charge he had laid on Damir had only fired his ambition. Pushed him to be who he needed to be, whatever the cost. It was worth it. The late lonely nights in the office or at his desk at home, the risky deals and the falling away from his friends were all worth it.

It had to be.

Lily leaned forward and placed a hand on

his arm, the warmth of her touch spreading through him. 'When your life falls apart, when everything you think you know disappears, it's hard to know how to make sense of it all.' Damir got the impression that she was speaking from experience. 'I don't know much about what happened here, about the war. I know that Josip left Croatia as soon as he could and has never returned. It makes sense that the war had a profound effect on your father as well, that it pushed him to take your grandfather's dream and do everything he could to make it happen. I'm sure he would be very proud of you.'

He shrugged. 'Maybe.' He'd never allowed himself to think about it. 'My grandfather died after we built the first hotel here, but he died knowing that we were on our way. And then my father was head of the family and he wanted more and more. One hotel wasn't enough, two wasn't enough. I don't know how many would have been, if there was a moment he would have thought, yes, we're here. I did it.'

'When did he die?'

'Eight years ago.' Now it was her turn to clasp his hand, her warmth offering comfort. 'I'd been married for a little over a year. Kata had her first teaching job, she liked me home in the evenings, liked to spend weekends with me...'

'That doesn't sound like too much to ask.'

'For someone else, maybe not. But she knew who I was when she married me, knew my family and our ambitions.' He looked out at the sea, remembering the pressure of those days, torn between two people he loved. 'It wasn't easy, balancing her expectations with my own. She always felt I put her last, my father that I was uncommitted. He doubled his workload to show me up, although his doctor had been advising him to take things easier.'

The conversation had taken an unexpected personal turn. Somehow Lily's soft questions got through his carefully built defences. First, back in Dubrovnik, he had opened up about Kata, now here he was talking his father. Topics he never discussed, not with anyone.

He hesitated, but the next words spilled

out before he could stop them. 'He was here, overseeing the upgrade of the hotel, when he had a heart attack. Overseeing it because I had taken the day off to take Kata sailing.' Sometimes he thought that day out with Kata had been the last day of peace he'd known. 'It took too long for the air ambulance to come. He was dead on arrival at the hospital. My mother blamed the hotel, blamed Lokvar, blamed me.'

'And do you blame yourself?'

How could he not? 'I should have been here.'

Her grip tightened as if she were trying to imprint her words onto him. 'It was the weekend. You were with your wife where you had every right to be and your father disregarded his doctor's instructions. It's very sad but no one's fault. Especially not yours.'

But he knew better. He was responsible and that knowledge was a burden he'd never be able to shed—neither did he deserve to. 'I knew what he was like. I just didn't want to let him win. He was a proud, stubborn bastard. I guess that's one thing I inherited from him. So I promised him

I wouldn't let him down. Not again. And I haven't. I've achieved far more in the years since he died than he could ever have dreamed.' But it wasn't enough. He wasn't sure it ever would be. But developing this land, achieving his father's dearest dream here might just give him the closure he craved.

Lily looked at him keenly, and then got to her feet. 'Come on,' she said, pulling his hand. He didn't move and she tugged him again. 'Come on.'

'Where?'

'It's Saturday night, I've been working hard all day and I don't know about you but I feel like I deserve a treat. The island band are playing down at the harbour and although I would never have thought I'd say this, I'm getting quite partial to their unique brand of rock covers of European pop. So let's go and dance.'

'Dance? Oh, no. I don't dance.'

'Sure you do, you just choose not to. I usually choose not to as well, but this evening I am planning to.' She smiled then, pleadingly. 'Don't make me dance alone, Damir.'

She wouldn't be alone for long. Not while she stood with big eyes blazing with hope, her hair falling silk-like down her back, long legs encased in shorts. Possessiveness seized him as he rose to his feet. 'You might regret this,' he warned her. 'No one has ever accused me of having rhythm before.'

'I won't judge you if you won't judge me,' she promised. 'Come on.'

He knew what she was doing. Trying to take his mind off the past, to lighten the mood, and it was working. Damir couldn't remember the last time he'd socialised on Lokvar, spent an evening in his own bar as a guest, not the manager, but to his surprise he realised he was actually looking forward to it. To spending the evening with Lily by his side. Just as if this was nothing but the summer affair he had offered her. And for a moment he wished that this was all it was. No business, no agenda, just attraction and fun.

Maybe it could be. For tonight at least.

CHAPTER SEVEN

THE MUSIC WAS LOUD, pounding through the bar, as the band added extra bass and percussion to last year's Europop breakout hit. Lily tossed her hair and twirled, any pretensions to rhythm and co-ordination long gone. Damir on the other hand hadn't been entirely honest when he had claimed to be no dancer, moving in a sinuous pattern that turned her whole body molten with lust.

He was an enigma, one she desperately wanted to puzzle out. Carelessly handsome, seemingly easygoing, the sheer scale of his success and the shortness of the timescale in which he'd achieved that success pointed to a man who was neither careless nor easygoing. And behind his flirtatious smile lay a man scarred by the failure of his marriage and his father's death. Scars she sensed he let very few if any people see.

Like her he seemed to be surrounded by acquaintances rather than friends, although he had grown up in this small tight-knit community. Only she had been lucky enough to have Izzy. Since his divorce she sensed that Damir had been almost entirely alone. Was that distance self-imposed or had it grown along with his success?

So why was he so open with her? Maybe because she was safe, leaving in just a couple of months. Or maybe because of the connection between them, unexpected but palpable.

A physical connection, a searing attraction, nothing more. Yet with every conversation, every touch, every glance she felt it sink further in, deeper and deeper, lodging within her. She wanted him, yes, more and more as the evening went on. But she wanted to know *him*, all of him. She'd never felt like this before, this out-of-control need. It terrified her and exhilarated her in equal measure. Control was so much part of her, built into her every thought and deed, her safety net and guidance. Yet here she was, dancing with no control at all with a man she barely knew, a man she wanted more and more with every passing moment. So much so that when she had gone upstairs to change her top and shoes and brush her hair before they had headed to the bar, she'd opened the pack of condoms she kept in her wash bag more out of habit—always sensible, always prepared—than any expectation of needing them. She could feel the outline of the foil packet in her back pocket, sure everyone could see it and know what she was thinking. Hoping. Wanting.

'Having fun?' Damir slipped an arm around her waist and pulled her close. No one took any notice. Their relationship seemed to be common knowledge already, thanks to the small island's extremely efficient grapevine, so Lily wound her arms around his neck and pressed closely against the hardness of his body, swaying in time with him.

'I am. Thank you for coming, it wouldn't have been so much fun on my own.'

'Thank you for asking me. It's been a long, long time since I spent a Saturday night here, but I'm having a good time.'

'As good a time as at a fancy restaurant in Dubrovnik?'

'It isn't the place that matters, it's the company. I'd still like to take you to that restaurant, though, show you my home.'

'Was that the plan? To invite me back for coffee?' she teased, pressing closer. He closed his eyes briefly as she moved against him, visibly swallowing, and the thrill of the effect she was having on him shuddered through her.

'Absolutely.' He bent his head and captured her mouth with his, a swift searing kiss that buckled her knees. 'Want to go for a walk?' His voice was ragged.

'I remember what happened last time you invited me for a walk,' she said, smiling up into his eyes and seeing heat flickering in their depths.

'Me too. Every second.'

'In that case let's go.'

Damir held her hand possessively as they slipped away from the bar and wandered back along the side of the harbour until they reached the path that bisected the island. This time Damir didn't take any diversions and fifteen minutes later they were back on the beach. The lights were still on at the beach bar and she could hear voices and music. Without speaking they turned the other way, making their way along the empty moonlit beach.

Lily took a long deep breath, inhaling the sweet sea air. 'There is nowhere like this, is there? I can't believe I get to live here, even if it's just for a while. I'm so glad I came, it wasn't an easy decision to make.'

'I'm glad you're here too.' Damir squeezed her hand and her whole body quivered. 'But I'm intrigued. What made a London lawyer decide to spend her summer serving beer and coffee to holiday-makers?'

'I make beds and dust too. Speak to demanding guests. I'm trying to arrange a wedding for a month's time and I have never had a client as difficult as this particular bride.'

'I don't pay my wedding planners enough for the problems they have to solve, I know that. It must be a reassurance for Marija to know you're looking after everything for her.'

'So Josip claims. But Ana can run the

B&B perfectly well without me, we all know that.' She paused. He'd been honest with her, shared more than she'd expected. Could she do the same? Should she? 'But really I'm here under a pretext.'

'Oh?'

'It's a stitch-up between my mother, Josip and Marija to get me away from London, to give me some space. And I agreed because they were right, I needed to get away. And I agreed because I'd made a promise to start living differently and this seemed as good a place to start as any.' Lily took a deep breath. She could feel her heart pounding, her chest sore; her grief physically hurt, weighing her down, and she couldn't bear the solitude of it any longer. 'My best friend died four months ago.'

The words were out. Lily's eyes burned as she heard imagined echoes reverberating around the cove. Every time she said the words it was with disbelief. It was all so absurd. With a jolt she realised Damir had stopped, taken her other hand, his clasp strong and comforting. 'I'm so sorry.'

'Thank you.'

'Would you like to tell me about her?'

She stared up at him. His face was shadowed in the moonlight but his voice kind, filled with sympathy. She couldn't have handled either before today, getting by with practicality and a hefty dose of denial, but his comforting hands holding hers, the lack of platitudes gave her the strength to nod.

'I would, if you're sure.'

'She was important to you, of course I'm sure.'

They carried on walking until they reached the rocks clustered at the end of the beach. Damir let go of her hands and began to climb up, and Lily could see an easy path through them. 'There's more sand on the other side of here,' he said. 'Like a private little beach.' Sure enough, a brief scramble later and they were sitting on a tiny horseshoe of sand encircled by the rocks, the dunes and the sea. She could see the lights from the villa on the other side of the bay, a few boats moored further out to sea. Otherwise it was as if they were alone in the world.

Lily clasped her knees in one hand and stared out at the dark water for a long, long time, memories jostling for attention.

'Izzy and I were really close,' she said at last. 'We were more like sisters than friends. And in some ways we were alike, although she was a lot more outgoing than me. Everyone loved her. She was so funny, and she would do anything for the people she loved.'

'Sounds like a good friend to have. Where did you meet?'

'At school. When mum married Josip I had to start a new school. I was shy anyway, and all the friendship groups had already been formed so I hid in the library every lunch and break. I soon realised I wasn't the only lower school girl hiding out in there, mostly because Izzy insisted on sitting with me and asking me a hundred questions. She should have been the lawyer, she was always wanting to know about everything and everyone. She was insatiably curious.' She closed her eyes and saw them, two girls in too-big uniforms, side by side at the wooden table, books spread out in front of them.

'Izzy could have been in any friendship group she wanted, but she didn't care about popularity. She was determined to get the highest grades in the school, to go to Oxford or Cambridge, she had it all planned out. She'd grown up in care, you see, lived with eight different foster families by the time I met her. Mum and Josip adored her, she was in a stable home by then or I think they would have taken her in.

'Looking back, I realise I was probably too dependent on her, I didn't look for other friends, didn't need them. Izzy knew everyone, and I followed where she led. But although she enjoyed a party, usually had some besotted boy hanging around, her real focus was on her future. We drew up life plans that first year we met. Oxford for me, Cambridge for her. Law for me, computers for her. Then good jobs, sharing a flat in London, promotions. By thirty I would be partner and she would have got the investment for her first start-up.'

She laughed, hearing it all said aloud. 'It sounds ridiculous, doesn't it, but we had a whole timetable. And we stuck to it. Thought it was worth it, even though we missed out on a lot of rites of passage.'

'Success takes sacrifice,' Damir said, and she nodded.

'And we sacrificed. Especially after university. We never took the time to go to the beach on a sunny day, never travelled, barely took a full weekend off. We always thought we had all the time in the world once we'd got to where we needed to be. But we were wrong. Izzy didn't have all the time, her time was cut short.'

'Did she have a boyfriend?'

Lily laughed. 'Izzy attracted attention wherever she went, but when you're always cancelling plans to work, boyfriends don't tend to hang around too long. We were getting to the stage where we saw friends start to get engaged, a couple had babies, but neither of us wanted that kind of baggage, not yet. Izzy once said that she thought thirty-two was the right age to start thinking about marriage. It sounds silly, doesn't it? Our lives. All planned out and on track.

'But Izzy dying at twenty-eight wasn't in the plans, not at all. And then I realised we were so busy living for the future we'd forgotten to live at all.' Her voice faded to a whisper and Damir squeezed the hand he was still holding. She swallowed, the pain in her throat almost overwhelming.

'She always wanted children one day, a big family with a dog and a range cooker like in the adverts, she said, to make up for the family she didn't have. She wanted to foster herself, to give back. And she didn't get to do or have any of it. She was desperate to go to Costa Rica and see sloths, to travel up the Californian coast, to see Petra, but she never took the time and now she'll never go. So I promised her. I would start to live. For her as well as me. That's why I'm here. Trying to learn to be spontaneous, trying to have fun. To live.'

Lily's hand was warm and soft in his. Damir couldn't, wouldn't let it go. He'd never heard anyone sound so lonely, sound so desolate before and shame filled him for how he'd tried to probe to find out her family secrets, how he'd tried to use her. She deserved more than to be a pawn in his power games, she deserved to be loved and cherished. To be desired.

And, oh, how he desired her. That was no deceit.

'You must be the bravest woman I know,' he said, and she turned to face him, eyes wide with surprise.

'Brave? Me?'

'Coming to a place where you know nobody, where you don't speak the language, to do a job you have no idea how to do. To leave your family and job, your whole life behind. That's pretty brave.'

'Well,' she said a little shakily, 'when you put it like that, I guess it was a little brave. To be honest, none of it comes easily, I spend an awful lot of time thinking, *What would Izzy do?*'

'Do you speak to her?'

'All the time. Does that sound silly?'

'Not at all.' He paused. 'I speak to Dad, tell him my plans.'

'It's a way of keeping them with us,' Lily said softly. 'A way to carry on without them. There's a hole in my life, and it will always be there. I'll marry someone she will never meet, if I have children they will never know her. No one will ever know the me she knew. The insecurities she knew. No one will remember the way I cried over my first boyfriend even though I told everyone he was getting in the way of my studies, or how hard I worked for my A+ in maths. No one else was there when I got offered a place at my first-choice firm and danced around the kitchen.

'I told her everything. She was the most kindred of kindred spirits and now she's not here. I can't just stop talking to her.' She smiled shakily. 'What do you say to your father? Do you ask his advice?'

'Advice, no. I tell him what is going on. Report in, I suppose.'

'Making sure you're on track?'

'Making sure I exceed expectations, keep my promise,' he corrected her, and she shifted a little so she faced him, her hand still warm in his. Anchoring him, grounding him.

'They hold a lot of weight, those promises to those who are no longer here. But believe me when I tell you that your promises are meaningless, your success meaningless if you don't take the time to just be occasionally. To live. To make memories. It took a lot for me to agree to sit with you at the party, to go to Dubrovnik. I wanted to hide behind my work at the villa, just as

I always had. But I knew that I needed to make some memories.'

'Is that why you're here? Collecting memories?'

'I hope so. But at the moment I am trying to live in the moment, to be spontaneous. To feel.'

He had no idea who made the first move. One moment they were sitting side by side, their hands linked, the next she was in his arms and his mouth was on hers. This was no sweet, gentle exploratory kiss, this was an incendiary kiss full of urgency and need and pent-up frustration. There was no gentle exploration of bodies, no careful learning or touch.

Instead Lily impatiently pulled at his shirt, tugging it over his head still half-buttoned, her hands immediately sliding down to unbutton his shorts. He was no less busy, slipping her T-shirt off, inhaling sharply at the touch of her silky bare skin under his hands as he slid his hands across the back of her bra until he found the clasp, undoing it and tossing the garment to one side.

Damir hissed as Lily finally undid his

trouser button, beginning to push his trousers down around his hips, all his blood rushing to that same spot with deep, primal urgency. 'Not so fast,' he managed, capturing her hands in his, stilling her progress.

'Why not?' she gasped, and Damir smiled, slowly and with intent against the sweetness of her mouth, edging back until he was leaning against the rocks and pulling her onto his knees so she knelt astride him, kissing her again, deep and hungry and so intoxicating he lost all knowledge of who and where he was.

'Because we've barely got started,' he told her after a moment, and chuckled at her whimper. With a Herculean effort Damir slowed things down, grazing his way down her neck, biting softly into the sweet hollow there until she moaned, throwing her head back to give him better access. He carried on exploring, his lips moving over the softness of her breasts while he carefully, slowly undid her shorts, sliding them down her thighs, stroking the soft skin beneath in slow, intent circles that mirrored his kisses, his fingers gliding up by infinitesimal steps until he found the very core of her.

She jolted as he touched her, then settled, moving in time with him. Damir's lips found hers as he continued to stroke her until, with a small cry, she came apart against him, falling into him with shuddering breaths. Damir held her close as her breathing settled, his own pulse beating wildly, the scent of her enveloping him until Lily pulled away, cupping his face with her hands.

'I haven't…' He managed to steady his voice. 'I wasn't expecting this, I'm not prepared.'

Lily smiled, reaching back into her shorts pocket and pulling out a small square package. 'Luckily for you, I am…unless you don't want to?'

It was hard to breathe, hard to function with his blood pulsing, with every instinct urging him forward. Damir reached out and took the packet from her unresisting fingers and drew Lily back towards him. 'Oh, I do want. I want very much. Would you like me to show you how much?'

'Yes please,' she breathed, and then she

was kissing him again and everything and everyone disappeared. There was just her, and for now she was all that he needed or wanted. For the first time in a really long time tomorrow could take care of itself.

CHAPTER EIGHT

'Was it worth the wait?'

Lily waited until the waiter had finished clearing their plates and left the table before she answered. 'Honestly? I thought nothing would beat fresh pizza overlooking the sun setting on Fire Bay, but you have managed it. This place was *definitely* worth the wait. I just can't believe the setting.'

'There's a reason it's one of Dubrovnik's most sought-after restaurants.' A smug smile played around Damir's mouth but, she conceded, he had a right to be smug. She had never been anywhere like this in her life. The restaurant was actually *on* the old town's city walls, the intimate tables adjoining the parapets so that diners could sit and look out across the Adriatic whilst enjoying the exquisite tasting menu. Damir was on first-name terms with the waiters, and they had been steered to the very best table, in a private corner with stunning views all around.

'Thank you for the loveliest day, I feel very spoiled.'

To be fair Lily didn't just *feel* spoiled, she *was* being spoiled. Damir had pulled out all the stops for their postponed date, sailing her across to Sunset Bay on the Lapad Peninsula, a bustling tourist resort just outside Dubrovnik. They'd walked around the beautiful headland, popping into a bar built into a cave for a coffee before enjoying a swim from the bar's bathing platform. Sunset Bay offered a very different holiday experience from Lokvar, with its myriad hotels catering for everyone from backpackers to luxury seekers.

A vibrant, café-filled boardwalk offered visitors a cornucopia of dining and drinking choices, with music pumping from several bars, screens showing sports and sales booths tempting visitors with various excursions along the coastline and out to the islands. By contrast, Lokvar was sleepy and slow, and Lily was only just beginning to realise just how much she loved the island and its laid-back pace.

'You deserve spoiling, especially after all those breakfast shifts,' Damir said, and she laughed.

'Breakfast, lunch and dinner. No wonder Marija is so fit, there is no gym programme that can burn as many calories as I have managed to burn over the last few days. The waitress work out with optional chambermaid cardio. I highly recommend it, I've never had such definition in my arms.' She flexed one for him to admire and he reached out to squeeze it, the caress softening as he ran a finger down her bare arm. Lily half closed her eyes as sensation rippled through her. How could one light touch leave her needing more in this way?

'Would you like to order coffee?' The waiter was back, and Damir looked enquiringly at Lily.

'Coffee? Or would you like to come back to my place for a nightcap?' The words were innocuous enough but the playful gleam in Damir's eyes told her he hadn't forgotten their conversation on the beach just before they had made love for the first time.

'A nightcap sounds nice,' she said as nonchalantly as she could, while every nerve fired up in anticipation. 'I'm happy to go back to your place if it's easier.'

A wolfish grin spread across his face and the anticipation intensified. 'Then let's go.'

It took less than five minutes for Damir to pay, waving away Lily's attempts to do so, before escorting her along the road. They'd travelled to Lapad by boat, then moored in the old harbour where they'd moored last time she'd visited the city, and Lily had expected that they would return there and sail to Damir's home. Instead they left the Old Town by a different gate and he led her along a wide promenade overlooking the sea. Villas and hotels were set back behind imposing gates and lush green gardens on either side, and he stopped at one gate, keying in a code so that it swung open.

'You live here?' She eyed the gracious stone building in some surprise. It was clearly old, at least a hundred years old, stately with its shuttered windows and pretty balustraded balconies fronted by neat lawns and cypress trees. She'd been expecting something modern and sleek and soulless, all glass and steel and cutting edge, not this beautiful piece of history.

'Do you approve?'

'I… On first impressions, yes, but I'll need to look around first,' she said. 'I have no idea about your taste in decor yet. You can't expect me to judge sight unseen.'

She needn't have worried. The villa more than lived up to its promise thanks to high ceilings, curving staircases and polished wooden floors. An enormous kitchen diner dominated the back of the house, sliding doors opening onto a huge flower-filled terrace furnished with a table and chairs and comfortable loungers. Steps led down to a swimming pool and hot tub nestled into the cliff side, the sea far below.

The decor was plain but clearly expensive, original pieces of modern art on the walls and some beautiful glass sculptures cleverly displayed. But there were no personal effects, no photos, no left-out books or notes, not even an unwashed mug in the sink. It was a beautiful house, but it wasn't a home. It could be one of his holiday lets, rather than the place in which he lived.

It wouldn't take much, she mused as she followed him around. Some family photos, a throw on the pristine, stylish sofa, a cosy armchair in the bay window, some bright rugs. And people. This was a house made for a family, not a man who spent most of his time elsewhere.

'You are so lucky to live in a beautiful place,' she said, once they were sitting on the terrace with the promised coffee and a glass of Croatian walnut brandy. The terrace was lit by subtle lowlights all around, candles burning on the table in front of them. The air was sweet and flower scented, birds calling from the trees all around. It was so peaceful they might have been in the middle of the countryside, not the centre of a bustling city. 'Have you been here long?' Maybe he'd just moved in. That would explain the lack of personal effects.

'I bought it for Kata, she always wanted to live in one of these houses. But she left before we could move in.'

'You kept it?'

'Why not? It's central. Close to the harbour, to the business district, to the main road.' This was all true, but she still felt that this should be a family home with its large rooms and many bedrooms, not an austere bachelor pad. 'And I feel at peace here,' he added, his voice so low she barely heard him. 'Sitting here, looking out to sea at the horizon and the water. It renews me.'

'I think I understand,' Lily said softly, trying to reconcile this admission with the self-confessed workaholic he was. 'It is restorative, isn't it? Not just the view but the air, the silence—I can feel my soul reviving just sitting here. Although I suppose that could be the brandy.'

'What about you? Where is home for you? Where are you at peace?'

Home. There was a concept. Not in her apartment, as soulless and modern as she had expected Damir's to be. Not even the small Ealing terrace where her mother and Josip lived.

The only place where she had ever felt anything like the peace Damir described was in Lokvar, and she was only a temporary resident there. 'In a way I've been looking for a home all my life, but in another way I think it's safer not to have one, because then you can't lose it.'

Where had *that* come from?

'Lose it?' Surprise flashed in his eyes as he turned to look at her.

'We moved around a lot when I was a kid,' she said as offhandedly as she could. 'My mother was a bit of a traveller. As soon as I was settled in one place we'd be on the move, until she met Josip, that is. They've stayed put since they got married. They don't even really go on holiday.'

'That must have been difficult.'

'It was all I knew, you know what kids are like. Adaptable.' She fixed a bright smile onto her face. 'It was a long time ago. Ancient history.'

'Not that ancient if you're still searching for a place where you feel safe,' he said gently.

'I do feel safe,' she protested. 'People make me feel safe, they make a home, not a place. Josip, Izzy… I guess that's why I am struggling so much. I haven't just lost my friend, I've lost part of me.'

'And your mother? Does she not make you feel safe?'

Lily bit her lip, old habits of loyalty making it hard to be honest. 'That's a big question. I do love her, I love her a lot. But she was really young when she had me for a start, not yet eighteen, and totally not ready for a baby.'

'Just a child herself.'

'I understand that now. My goodness, when she was my age she had an eleven-year-old. It must have been hard. I do see that.'

'And your father?'

'Unknown. That's what it says on my birth certificate and that's what she's always said—that's the problem when you're conceived at a seven-day-long rave during the second summer of love. You try tracking down a man whose name she can't remember from thousands of attendees. My grandparents were kind of strict and Mum really rebelled against that, was always running away to raves and festivals. And then, once I was born, she just took me with her.

'Some of my earliest memories are of

hanging out at a festival with anyone sober enough to take care of me. She lived in squats or travelled around in vans, we crashed with friends or lived in communes. Sometimes there were boyfriends, some more long term than others, a few better than others, but none that could be thought of as any kind of father figure. It was chaotic.'

Saying the words aloud brought it back. The constant change and uncertainty. The days or weeks when there was no money, the mornings her mother didn't wake up at all.

She took another sip, staring out to sea but not seeing anything but the past. 'When I was ten my grandparents took me away and I lived with them. They were very keen to make sure I didn't turn out like Mum. Very strict, it couldn't have been more of a contrast.'

'That must have been really hard.' His voice was gentle, the chill of his earlier words gone.

'Yes and no. I missed her so much, but all I wanted to do was live in one place and have a normal life. No more parties, no more changing schools or missing school.' She paused, remembering the relief mixed with the pain of missing a mother who had barely noticed her absence. 'But my grandparents didn't really want me, I was a duty, and I knew it.'

'So what happened?'

'Mum overdosed. She nearly died. Josip was the paramedic who saved her. A year later she was sober, they were married and I went to live with them. She went to university, became a social worker. She's amazing, I am so proud of her. Josip changed her life and he changed mine. I'll always be so grateful to him. But I suppose part of me will always remember what it's like not being able to depend on the people who are supposed to look out for you. I look at Mum and Josip, they are so happy, they have this perfect partnership and I want that closeness and trust. But I don't think it's in me.

'I don't trust people not to leave. Izzy did, she didn't mean to but she did.' She stared at him in horror, covering her mouth with her hands as if she could push the words back. 'I didn't mean…'

'It's okay to mean it. Anger is part of grief. There's no one way to miss someone, one way to feel.'

'We were supposed to be friends all our lives,' she whispered. 'What if no one else ever knows me the way she did? What if I'm alone for ever?'

'Hey,' he rose to his feet in one graceful moment and walked around the table, pulling her to her feet and tilting her chin so she met his gaze. 'You are loyal and funny and kind and there are lots of people out there who would love to be part of your life if you let them.'

'You think?'

'I know,' he told her. His gaze darkened as it moved to her mouth and she was aware how close they were, every part of her pressed up against him. She looked up at him, lips parted, breathless, expectant, needing until he finally claimed her mouth with his. His kiss was gentle, weakening her with its sweetness as he explored her mouth unhurriedly, the tenderness in his kiss melting her. His arms slipped around her, keeping her close, but made no attempt to touch her further, to reach under her clothes, to move them onto the next stage in this particular age-old dance. This was a kiss for kissing's sake and all the more potent for it.

Lily rose onto her tiptoes, better to lean in, entwining her arms around his neck, pulling Damir closer, luxuriating in the feel of his mouth and hands, savouring every sensation. Time slid away, all she knew was him, the taste of him, the feel of him, his muscles under her hands, his light touch on her waist, those clever, sinful lips and the feelings they sparked shooting through her, weakening her.

'Damir...' Lily half moaned, wanting more, and yet at the same time not wanting this gentle seduction to end. He didn't answer in words but deepened the kiss, starting to demand, to taste, to make clear his want, and she responded in kind, wiggling closer, her body pressed against his. She tangled her hands in his hair, pulling him closer still, and Damir groaned against her mouth, his hands finally, finally beginning to move, sliding down to her hips to move her against him, backing her up until she hit the table.

'This isn't the most comfortable place to do this. We could take it inside.' He hesitated. 'If you want, you can stay. You're not working tomorrow morning, are you?'

'Is this your usual line?' Lily half joked, resorting to humour as she tried to process what had happened, her confession followed by the sweetest kiss she had ever experienced. 'Nightcap on the terrace then move it upstairs for a sleepover?'

Damir was silent, and she felt his body rigid against hers. 'No,' he said at last. 'I have dated many women since my divorce, yes. I've had sex with some of those women, always monogamously, always carefully. But I've never invited any of them to spend the night here. I sleep alone. You will be the first.'

She had no idea how to process that information. No idea what it meant. But Lily understood that the invitation was more than casual. That for Damir to ask her stay in a place that was obviously his sanctuary was a privilege. That for him to make himself vulnerable enough to ask her to stay was a gift, one she couldn't easily turn down. 'In that case I'd be honoured.'

'Are you sure?' The question seemed loaded. As if he was asking her about more than her agreement to stay the night, and she held his gaze as she answered. The next step Lily knew, was down to her and she thrilled with the power he entrusted in her.

'I'm sure,' she said. She leaned back and looked up at him fearlessly, her whole body tingling at the intensity in his dark gaze.

She led the way, wiggling out of their close embrace and walking as confidently, as provocatively as she could to the open doors that led into the villa. Damir stood by the table, one white-knuckled hand gripping it as he watched her, heat dancing in his eyes. Not breaking his gaze, Lily stepped inside, every nerve alight with trembling desire and need.

She walked through the kitchen diner to the tiled hall and slowly, purposefully up the curving staircase until she reached the wide landing and continued down it. Damir's room was at the far end, a corner suite overlooking the sea.

She didn't falter but turned the handle to open the door, pulling her dress above her head as she did so and discarding it on the floor. With one quick movement she unclasped her bra, discarding it likewise, and wiggled out of her underwear. Pulling the top sheet off the bed, she climbed in, resisting the temptation to cover herself. Instead she half turned to face the door, leaning up on one elbow, her legs curved behind her, and watched Damir stop at the door of the room.

With satisfaction she heard his intake of breath as he saw her waiting for him, his eyes travelling over her in excruciatingly slow detail, as if he were touching her remotely. Lily had never felt so powerful, never felt so beautiful, never felt wanted the way she felt wanted right now. The hunger in Damir's face was a gift, a homage to her, and she gloried in it.

He stood, holding her gaze as he disposed of his own clothes. Tall, powerful and, oh, so sexy it took less than two strides for him to join her.

'What took you so long?' she managed to say.

Damir cupped her face and stared at her for one long, endless moment. 'You're so beautiful,' he said hoarsely, before his mouth took hers in a searing kiss that made Lily forget who she was, where she was, forget everything but the sensations pulsing through her.

All she knew was the feel of this man under her hands as she tried to learn every part of him, the play of the muscles on his back, the strength in his arms, the delicious subtleness of his touch, the way he made her gasp, the way he made her yearn and want, teasing and giving until all she could do was call out his name, biting down on his shoulder, tasting him and knowing him, giving as she received.

But at the back of her mind, as with one delicious movement he joined them as one, Lily was aware of an extra intensity in her, an awareness that her response wasn't just provoked by the day they'd shared, by the chemistry between them, by the undoubted skill of his lovemaking. She could tell herself all she wanted that this was a summer fling, but her response to him was fuelled by emotion. She had no reason to trust him, every reason to remember that this was just a game they played, but as she held onto him and allowed the sensation to carry her away, Lily tried to block out the realisation that she might just be falling for him.

CHAPTER NINE

LILY FIDGETED NERVOUSLY as the boat sailed around the headland, Dubrovnik lit up in the distance, pulling her wrap more closely around her shoulders although the early evening air was warm. She felt a little uncomfortable, the only passenger on the charter boat Damir had sent to collect her, although she had insisted she would have been fine jumping on one of the open-topped passenger ferries that connected Lokvar with the mainland. The driver of the small speedy boat hadn't spoken to her beyond a few grunts, leaving her alone with her thoughts.

And she had a lot to think about, two emails that day jolting her from the contented haze that had enveloped her the last few weeks as she had spent her days either working or spending time with Damir—

time that was becoming increasingly important to her. She pulled at her wrap impatiently. How she wished he had picked her up so she could discuss her news and thoughts through with him.

Damir had asked her to accompany him to the opening ceremony of the Summer Festival, a six-week celebration of arts and culture that encompassed the whole area—Lokvar would be hosting a theatre company who would perform several times a week in the small but idyllic botanical gardens. The opening ceremony, a concert, was by invitation only, followed by a champagne reception.

To be there with Damir felt like a huge jump from barbecuing at his villa or hanging out on Lokvar, where everyone knew them, and at the back of her mind she couldn't help wondering what this very public stepping out meant. Probably nothing as a quick internet search had shown her photos of Damir at lots of high society occasions, always with a perfectly groomed companion, rarely the same one twice.

Women who had agreed to the same caveat of short, sweet and finite as she had.

But did they also find themselves forgetting those conditions, falling deeper with every conversation? Probably not, they seemed like the kind of women who didn't just know the rules but made the rules, while Lily was figuring it all out as she went.

It didn't help that the evening would also be a huge test of Lily's nerves. Big formal occasions always intimidated her, although she tried her best to hide it. Especially big formal occasions where she didn't know anyone. She knew Damir was there to be seen, to circulate. The opening ceremony was an important night in the Dubrovnik social calendar.

At least she had managed to find an appropriate outfit, a silver maxi dress and matching wrap that managed to look smart and feel comfortable. She'd left her hair loose but pulled back off her face and she wore the turquoise necklace and earrings Josip and her mother had given her for her twenty-first birthday.

This time, rather than the long sea journey round to the old harbour, she found herself taken to the much closer, but much less picturesque City Port, where several mid-size cruise ships were moored, along with hundreds of boats ranging from small dinghies to luxury ocean-going yachts. A car was waiting to whisk her to Pile, the entrance to the Old Town where Damir waited for her.

Lily's stomach fluttered as she took him in, sharply smart in a suit that had obviously been made for him, every line enhancing his tall, lean strength. His hair was slicked back and he was freshly shaved, smarter than she had ever seen him. Almost like a stranger, a reminder that for all their lovemaking, the confidences they had shared, she barely knew him at all.

'How was the journey?' His mouth grazed her cheek, lingering just a second too long for a polite greeting. 'Sorry I couldn't pick you up. My meeting overran.'

'That's okay, but I could have quite easily taken the ferry, you know.'

'I know.' He began to escort her through the now familiar gate that led into the Old Town, his hand proprietorial on her arm. Several other people, equally smartly dressed, called out greetings, looking curiously at Lily as they did so. 'But I promised to collect you and I always keep my word.'

'Good to know.'

The concert and ceremony were taking place in a square in the Old Town just outside St Blaise's church, the ancient building star of several films and television programmes. Seats had been erected in a square around a central stage and Damir escorted her to seats close to the front. The artists were beginning to tune up, the seats to fill, the whole square humming with excitement and anticipation. This concert would be broadcast live so the whole city could hear it, and would be followed by what she had been assured were spectacular fireworks.

'I'm sorry I didn't answer your call earlier,' Damir said once they were settled. 'Is everything okay?'

'Everything's fine, I just had a couple of emails today that I wanted to talk to you about. The first one was from the bride's family about the wedding later this month.'

Damir groaned. The whole B&B had been booked out the week after next for a wedding party. The wedding itself was due to take place in Dubrovnik, but all the guests would be staying at the B&B for a long weekend, arriving on the Thursday evening and leaving on the Monday. As the bride and groom's families were English, Lily had offered to deal with them, and as the wedding approached it seemed to take up a great deal of her time—and her conversation.

By now she was sure that Damir was as sick of them as she was.

The bride's demands had become increasingly onerous over the last few weeks, along with an ever-changing list of guest allergies and needs. Her demands had culminated in a sudden desire for separate dinners and entertainment for both the bride's and the groom's families and friends the evening before the wedding itself, both to be held at the B&B but not within sight of each other.

'Why can't one of them go over to the mainland?' Ana had grumbled when that particular request had come through, and although Lily had been too busy trying to work out just how they were going to accommodate it given the size of the villa to join in the grumbling, secretly she couldn't help but agree with her friend.

'No, what does she want now? For you to decorate the beach in her theme colours? An entire change of menu? Or does she want you to whip up several wedding dresses for her to choose from when she gets here?'

'No.' Lily laughed, though none of those suggestions would have surprised her. 'Much worse. They've split up, the wedding is off.'

'One of them has had a lucky escape, I can't help suspecting it's the groom.'

'I agree, but obviously they've cancelled completely and the bride's family are insisting on getting their deposit back. So that's been fun.'

'I take it you have told them just what they can do with that suggestion.'

'Several times. It hasn't stopped them trying, though. I've had the bride's mother and father and even her aunt on the phone all telling me just how they'll ruin me with bad reviews.' She sighed. 'The annoying thing is that Marija wouldn't usually allow the villa to be booked out for one event at the height of summer, but the groom's family are regulars so we agreed as a favour.'

'Does that mean there was no contract?'

'You forget who you're talking to. I wrote that contract and they agreed to a completely non-refundable fifty per cent deposit. So they can huff and puff all they want but they won't get a penny. But this means we're going to be empty at the height of summer, to say nothing of all the orders we are now going to have to cancel, and the boxes of favours and decorations we'll have to send back to the UK. I've ten boxes of champagne arriving tomorrow, the rest of the wine later in the week, and Antun's food order needed its own delivery boat.'

'You won't be empty for long,' Damir said. 'At this time of year there are always last-minute bookings and walk-ins.'

'That's what Ana said.' Lily looked down at her hands. 'But, you see, that Thursday is Izzy's birthday. I was relieved we were going to be so busy that it meant I wouldn't have time to brood. I need to make sure I stay busy. Or celebrate her in some way. Because I had a second email today. One that is much bigger in the grand scheme of things, much more unexpected. I could really do with your thoughts on it, because I am all over the place.'

'What is it?' His voice was low, reassuring, and she leaned in gratefully.

'Izzy's lawyer, the one dealing with her estate, got in touch. I knew that Izzy had left everything to me, but I didn't realise just what that meant.' She could hear the pitch of her voice rising and took a deep breath. 'What am I supposed to do with it all? What was she thinking?'

'It was more than you expected?'

She nodded, biting her lip to keep back the threatened tears. 'So much more. You see, she was a computer genius, worked for a couple of the really big firms. More than once she was headhunted for roles in Silicon Valley but she always turned them down. She liked to be rooted, she said. I guess that's what happens when you grow up with no roots at all.

'Anyway, I knew she was well paid, but it turns out that she had well over a million saved up. A million pounds! She could have bought her own house rather than sharing with me, begun the start-up she was planning, done anything. Instead she just kept saving.' She stared unseeingly at the stage and the musicians still warming up. 'I wonder what she meant to do with it. All the things she could have done and never did...' Her voice trailed off.

'And now it's yours?'

'I suppose so. Legally, yes. But, Damir, it doesn't feel right. Her books, the couple of paintings she acquired, her clothes even, they are different. I can accept them and remember her every time I see them or wear them. But a sum of money like this? I can't take it! It doesn't seem right.'

There was a lot she could do with such a huge sum of money. Pay off her mortgage, go travelling and have a huge nest egg for when she returned. Start her own business or put it aside, as Izzy had done, for her own rainy day and hope hers would actually arrive. This money gave her freedom, but it also weighed her down. It didn't seem right to squander it, it didn't seem right to use it at all. She too was well paid, she had savings of her own. She turned to Damir.

'What do you think I should do?'

* * *

Before Damir could answer the audience hushed and a few moments later the strains of a violin filled the air. Usually music had the power to transport him, no matter if it was classical, rock or something in between, but tonight he barely heard a note. Instead he was all too aware of Lily, straight-backed next to him, absorbed in the music, her last words echoing round and round.

'What do you think I should do?'

Why did his opinion matter? They weren't friends or confidants, they were lovers, enjoying a brief amount of time together before going their separate ways. Lily's future was nothing to do with him. Spend the money, give it away, what did he care?

Only he did care. He wanted to help her make sense of this new development, just as he wanted to help her deal with the bridal party's cancellation. He wanted to take all her cares and concerns and shield her from them.

And that wasn't in their agreement at all.

He clapped politely, a second after the

rest of the audience, relieved when a second piece started up, leaving him to his thoughts. There was no rhyme or reason to the way he felt. Their arrangement was, like all his arrangements, temporary. She was leaving at the end of the summer. And even if she wasn't, there would be an expiry date on their time together. She wasn't Croatian, she didn't come from an influential family, and although she shared his work ethic, she didn't have the background to help him expand, to move his business up to the next level. He sensed that Lily would never be happy with a role as hostess and facilitator. And that was the kind of wife he needed.

Hang on a second. Wife? Where on earth had *that* come from? True, he was in his early thirties, true, he'd always meant to remarry one day—he had to, had to father some heirs if the family business was to continue. But not yet. Not to a woman he had known for less than two months and slept with a handful of times. His marriage to Kata had been a failure, and he'd known her all his life. If and when he married again, guaranteeing the success of that

marriage was one of his paramount consid-
erations. And the only way to do that was
through a mutual understanding of shared
goals and benefits. A contract, not an emotional journey.

He knew all this, yet somehow, during the last few weeks, he had relaxed
his vigilance and this was the result, his
mind wandering to forbidden places.
Which meant he needed to take some action now. He could still see Lily while she
was around, but maybe he'd better guard
against getting any closer. Guard against
saying too much, guard against showing
too much, guard against feeling too much.
Enjoyable dates and satisfactory lovemaking and no emotion. They were his estab-
lished rules. It would be best not to deviate
again.

Mind made up, he did his best to concentrate on the rest of the concert and to
enjoy the fireworks that lit up the Old
Town. He exerted himself, ensuring he
was at his most charming and flirtatious,
making Lily laugh and blush in equal measure, but he also made sure they didn't re-
sume their earlier conversation. No more

heartfelt confidences, no advice. Seduction and fun only. He'd been in danger of losing sight of the end game. Of the villa, of his plans for it. He needed to dazzle Lily, make her understand his vision, advocate for him, not allow her into his heart.

He refused to consider that maybe it was a little too late for that.

The following reception was an even more exclusive gathering in the Sponza Palace, just a short walk through the Old Town. Lily gasped as he ushered her into the candlelit room, with its stone arches and high ceiling. 'I just can't get over how old and beautiful everything is,' she said, turning slowly while Damir procured two glasses of champagne from a hovering waiter. 'Just look at those archways. It's so strange to be somewhere still so intact that makes you feel like you could be living any time in the last thousand years. London has a lot of history, but everything is being rebuilt at such a great rate it's impossible to imagine it in the nineteenth century, let alone the sixteenth.'

'Come on, I'll show you around.' He took her arm and started along the hallway, only to stop as an elegant woman in a fitted black cocktail dress turned to look at them speculatively, a flicker of disdain in her hooded gaze. His chest tightened as he took in the familiar eyes, so like his own, the immaculately coiled hair, the perfect make-up.

She nodded. 'Damir.'

'Majka,' he replied, then switched to English. 'May I introduce you to Lily Woodhouse. Marija's granddaughter,' he added meaningfully, and his mother's eyes widened. Was that an actual gleam of approval he saw in them? 'Lily, this is my mother.'

'How lovely to meet you,' his mother said in her careful English. 'How is Marija?'

'Very well, thank you.'

'Is she enjoying her travels?' So his mother knew all the island news, although she hadn't set foot there in eight years.

'Very much. She's now back in London with Mum and Josip.'

'Is she?' Damir asked. Did that mean her travels were over and she would return this season after all?

Lily turned to him with a smile. 'Didn't

I tell you? She's never seen England in summer so they are planning a few weeks away to show her some of the country and to try and prove to her that it isn't always grey.'

'That sounds delightful,' his mother said in a voice that suggested it was anything but, and he could feel Lily stiffen beside him.

'I think so. It's nice to meet you,' she added. There was a dignity in her bearing, a cool politeness in tone that he had never seen or heard in Lily before. A memory flashed of just a few weeks ago, sitting eating pizza, telling Lily about his father's death. 'She blames me,' he had said.

Did Lily remember? Looking at the suddenly glacial woman beside him, he knew she did. She remembered and she cared. The tightness in his chest eased as she slipped her hand through his arm, tilting her chin a little more.

'Do pass on my best wishes to your family,' his mother said, her bearing as regal as Lily's, and Lily inclined her head.

'Of course. Thank you.'

'It was nice to see you, Damir. You and—

Lily, is it?—must come over for dinner one night. Ask your PA to call mine and arrange it. Have a good evening.' And she was gone. Damir released a breath he hadn't even known he was holding.

'Get your PA to call hers? Seriously?' Lily was almost squeaking in indignation and to his surprise the last of his tension left him as he took in her reaction.

'She remarried into old money. Now she lives the kind of life she always wanted— charity committees, city functions. She keeps herself very busy. Those three homes don't run themselves, you know.' In fact, he realised, his mother lived exactly the kind of life he envisioned for his wife.

'Even so. I bet even the Queen doesn't expect her children to organise a family dinner through their PAs. Will you do it?'

'No,' he said slowly. 'There's no point. She has a new life, one that doesn't include me. She's only interested to hear what new deals I've made, where I'm expanding. To see if I can be of use.'

'I'm sorry.'

'Don't be. She's never been that family focussed. She married my father because she knew he was going places but she always felt she married beneath her—and never let him forget it. Life on Lokvar, as the wife of a man who liked to get stuck in and get his hands dirty, working behind his own bar or on the building sites, never really suited her. I think she's glad to have put it all behind her.'

'Well, she's the one missing out,' Lily said. 'She should be bursting with pride to have a son like you, she should be hounding you to be at every dinner so she can show you off, not fobbing you off without even an air kiss. Come on, you promised me a guided tour before we were interrupted.'

'Yes, I did. Come on, this way.' But as he showed Lily around the famous old building her words kept echoing through his mind, and he kept replaying the moment Lily had drawn herself up in coldly polite outrage. He didn't need defending, he was more than capable of looking after himself, but to know that someone else cared, someone thought him worthy of defending was something he hadn't felt in a very, very long time. One thing was becoming clear: he could tell himself to emotionally distance himself from Lily, he could tell himself that this was just an affair, but the truth was he was falling for her. Worst of all, he didn't want to change a thing.

CHAPTER TEN

DAMIR LOOKED UP from his laptop and grinned. 'Good morning,' he said appreciatively, looking Lily up and down, lingering on every curve and dimple. If there was anything sexier than a pretty girl, tousled with sleep and wearing a man's shirt, he had yet to see it.

'Good morning, I didn't mean to oversleep,' she said as she leaned over to bestow one sweetly chaste kiss on his cheek.

'You didn't, I was up early. Besides, this is the first time you've had more than a few hours off in weeks, you needed it.'

He, on the other hand, had been awake most of the night, all too aware of her slumbering beside him. All the reasons he should put some distance between them had rolled through his head over and over again, but he knew he wouldn't. More importantly, he couldn't. Luckily, Lily was still only here for the summer. The only thing really at risk was his heart. And until recently he had been pretty sure he no longer had one to risk.

'It was blissful.' She stretched, the shirt rising up her thighs in a way that made concentrating on work almost impossible. 'No breakfast shift! No carrying coffee to tables, so desperate for a gulp it takes everything I have not to stop en route and finish the pot. No having to be perky and friendly first thing. Don't get me wrong, I love being there so much more than I could ever have imagined, but I was getting to the stage where I would have considered selling my soul for a lie-in.'

'No soul required and…' he jerked his head towards the kitchen counter '…there's a fresh pot of coffee over there.'

'You are a wonderful man, do you know that?' Lily padded over to the place he'd indicated to pour a cup, then returned to the kitchen table, pulling out a chair to sit opposite him. 'Mmm, this smells delectable.'

This was the first time they had spent a morning together like this. On the occasions Lily stayed over she usually got up bright and early and either Damir took her back to Lokvar or she caught the ferry home. Coffee was quickly gulped, breakfast snatched. This morning was unusually domestic.

And to his surprise he liked it that way.

'So what are your plans for the rest of your day off?' he asked, and she leaned back in her chair, pushing her unbrushed hair off her face.

'I think I might explore. There's a nice walk around the City Port, up towards Lapad, with plenty of beach clubs and swimming spots along the way. Maybe a spot of shopping. What about you? Can you play hooky at all?'

'Not today,' he said, more regretfully than he would have imagined possible. 'I have several conference calls today, a site visit and a board meeting.'

'Fun, fun, fun,' she teased, and he laughed.

'I'd rather spend the day with you.' He meant it.

'To be honest, it might be good for me to spend some time alone. I had an idea last night and I need to mull it over.'

'What kind of idea?'

Lily sipped her coffee, her eyes bright with mingled emotions: excitement, happiness and a tinge of grief. 'I think I finally figured out what I want to do with Izzy's legacy. I know I only found out just how much money she left me yesterday, and the sensible, cautious part of me is warning me not to make such a huge decision on so little time and with so little research, so a day walking and swimming might help me figure out whether I want to explore it further. But it feels right, you know?'

Damir pushed his laptop away and reached for his own coffee. 'What feels right?'

'I want to help other children like Izzy.' Lily's words came tumbling out. 'Help foster carers like Janet, who looked after Izzy for her entire teen years. You know, literally dozens of children have passed through her hands. Some only stay a few nights, some like Izzy for much longer. Before Janet, Izzy lived in about eight homes, but Janet gave her the chance to stay at the same school for all her secondary education, to be settled. It was such a gift.'

'She sounds wonderful.' How could it be that some people had the capacity to care for so many children, when others, like his own mother, couldn't muster up enough affection for just one?

'She is! But it's not an easy life and it's hard to give the children she looks after things that other kids take for granted. Like holidays abroad, for instance.'

'I'd never thought of that before.' Damir donated liberally to several causes, some because it was expected, local hospitals and cultural centres, and a few secretly, ones closer to his heart, such as marine charities. But he had never thought about what he could do personally. The difference he could make with his money and influence.

'I am thinking of using Izzy's money to bring families like Janet's, foster families, on holiday to the B&B. I want to put three rooms aside in the school holidays for them to use free of charge and to pay for flights and transfers so there's no reason not to come. I want to make sure children like Izzy get the chance not just to have a beach holiday but to learn to swim, to sail, to paddle board. And more than that,

I'd like to be able to offer summer jobs to kids who have turned eighteen, who aren't sure what to do next, to give them an opportunity to spend some time abroad and learn some skills. The villa is so magical, Fire Cove is so peaceful and so beautiful, letting children like Izzy was experience it feels like the best birthday gift I could give her.'

'What does Marija say?' Damir asked, trying to process what Lily's plan meant for him and his plans, his promises.

She looked down at her coffee and inhaled. 'I haven't broached it with her yet. There's a lot to think about, to plan and to figure out before I do, but I would like to have an answer before Izzy's birthday. I don't want to be sad on that day. I want to try and celebrate her life the way we couldn't at her funeral. If I knew that I could make this work that would make a celebration so much easier.'

It was a great idea, Damir could see that, but to fulfil it meant the villa staying as it was—and that meant he would never make his father's dream come true. There had to be a middle way. 'It's a great idea, Lily, but you don't actually need the villa, do you? It's Lokvar, not the B&B itself that's important, so you could pay for these families to stay anywhere on the island. In fact, I could donate rooms at my hotel, it would be my privilege. And I could take on a couple of summer workers. I'd be happy to support you.' Why couldn't they both get what they wanted, what they needed?

'That's very generous of you,' Lily said slowly, the enthusiasm in her face dimming. 'And your hotels are lovely, but some of these children will have never been abroad before, some have quite complex needs, they'd probably prefer somewhere a little more homely. I mean, I get intimidated by all those pristine white walls and all that gleaming glass in your hotel. I'm not sure it would be the right environment. But I will give it some thought, of course. Thank you.'

Another thought occurred to him. 'Does this mean you're planning to stay on Lokvar?' He wanted her to say yes and no in equal measure. He hadn't planned for her to stay, the only way he could cope with his feelings for her was by knowing she would leave in just a few weeks. 'Marija is over seventy, she needed to take this year off. At some point she'll have to sell the villa if Josip doesn't want it. Like it or not, change is coming. Your plans are wonderful, but you need to think about the future. Accept my offer, that way you'll be able to help more people for as long as you need.'

'Well, I was thinking maybe I could buy the villa.' She peeped hopefully up at him. 'I feel at home there in a way I've never felt before. I don't even mind those breakfast shifts. What do you think?'

If he were a different man, if he was interested in a long-term relationship with Lily, if he was capable of one, then surely this would be fantastic news. But he wasn't that man. He was Damir Kozina with a promise to keep and a plan that didn't allow for a curveball like a bright-eyed English girl who set his pulse racing and his heart feeling emotions he couldn't afford to feel.

'But that would take all your money, surely, and then how would you pay for flights and everything else you want to provide? The season is short, remember. Besides, would you want to stay here for the rest of your life? A summer, sure, but wait until you see the island in winter. Just you and three hundred other people who have known each other all their lives. It can be a lonely existence, Lily.'

'I know, I know. At the moment it's just an idea.' If she was disappointed at his lack of enthusiasm at her suggestion she stay, she hid it well.

'It's a good idea,' he said honestly. 'And I meant it when I said I wanted to help. I have other hotels, other villas that might be just as suitable. Fire Cove is special, but the whole coastline is full of beautiful spots that might serve you just as well. Why don't we discuss it tonight? After you've had the day to think about it?'

'Yes, you're probably right,' she said. 'Right now it's just ideas and dreams, maybe we can plan it all out this evening. I'm going to go and take a shower. I'll see you in a bit.'

Lily stepped out of the shower and swathed herself in the huge, sumptuously soft towel she'd found folded in the en suite bathroom. She felt more herself, with caffeine back in her system and freshly washed hair. Ready for the day that lay ahead.

She'd been a little deflated by Damir's lukewarm if helpful responses to her idea. But she had to admit he had a point. One perfect summer wasn't the same as making a life out here. Ana went back to Zagreb once autumn hit and the island quietened down, and it wasn't as if Damir had promised her anything more than a good time. She shivered, pulling the towel closer around her.

Was she basing her potential future on the hope of the connection between her and Damir being more than a one summer thing despite no indication from him that he was considering that? More fool her.

The irony didn't escape her. She, cautious Lily Woodhouse, considering giving up her hard fought for career to live on an island because she'd fallen in love. The very thought was laughable. After all, she'd considered herself incapable of falling hard and fast for any man. Turned out she'd just not met anyone capable of igniting that kind of desire before. It had been easy to think passion was beyond her when she'd never allowed herself to really relax with a potential lover. And she hadn't, her guard always up, even with the handful of boyfriends she'd had before. No wonder none of the relationships had lasted, she'd kept so much of herself locked away, all that was real and vibrant.

She pulled a face at herself in the mirror. No more dark introspective thoughts. She'd planned a fun day of leisure and exploring and she was going to enjoy every moment. Be a tourist, take selfies and live in the moment.

Lily dressed quickly in a pretty pink sundress before slathering herself in sun cream, adding the bare modicum of make-up, just some tinted moisturiser, lip salve and mascara and running the hairdryer over her thick hair to take the worst of the wetness out of it. She'd already prepared a tote bag with a bikini and towel, her phone, sunglasses and purse. She needed nothing else.

Grabbing her tote bag, she exited the bedroom and headed back down the landing and stairs into the kitchen diner where she had left Damir. He wasn't there, his laptop also missing. Neither was he in the shaded part of the terrace where he sometimes worked.

Lily stood irresolute. She didn't want to leave without saying goodbye, making plans to meet up later.

She wandered back through the kitchen, peeking into the large sitting room to see if he was there before trying the book-lined study at the front of the house. She had hardly set foot in this room, only peeped in that very first evening when he'd given her the grand tour. The laptop was here on the large desk set against the far wall, along with a tablet and Damir's phone, but no sign of the man himself.

She looked around, impressed by the large sunny room. It was exactly the kind of study she would like for herself, with its filled bookcases, cosy stove for winter days and a leather sofa in the bay window.

A large square table stood in the middle of the room, unrolled plans neatly laid out, an architect's impression, finely detailed in 3D. Lily glanced at them with idle curiosity and her heart thumped with painful recognition. The meticulously rendered plans showed a grand hotel curving round a gentle bay facing out to sea. It was lavish with rooftop swimming pools, grand terraces and lushly curved architecture. The sandy beach showed a swish-looking beach club, small boats bobbing off a pier. It all looked extremely exclusive.

There were very few sandy beaches on this part of the Dalmatian Riviera, and the size of the cove, the hillside carefully rendered in what she assumed was exact scale, was all too familiar. She took another look, trying to block out all the buildings and concentrate on the topography instead. She could swear that it was Fire Cove. That the heart of the hotel was exactly where the B&B was…

'Lily, are you okay?'

She whirled round. Damir had obviously been swimming. He stood there, wet hair slicked back, drops still drying on his olive chest, a towel slung low around his hips. His gaze quickly dropped to the paper then back to her. 'Do you want some breakfast before you head out?'

'Damir, what are these?' She gestured towards the paper and he shrugged elegantly, but his expression was wary—wary and a little sad.

'Plans my architect drew up.'

'Where for? Damir, I'm not a fool,' she said, proud that her voice wasn't shaking because right now she felt exactly like a fool. A fool who had been played. More than played. Who had walked straight into a set-up. 'This is Fire Bay isn't it? You're the businessman Marija mentioned. The one who offered to buy the villa but only because he wanted to tear it down. You still want it and that's why you've been so persistent. Wanting to get to know me, show me around, buy me flowers, seduce me. Isn't it?'

Emotion flashed momentarily in his dark eyes and for one moment Lily could believe it was sorrow. 'Not seduce you,' he said levelly. 'That was never part of the plan, believe me.'

And just like that the rosy haze she'd been operating in evaporated. How could she believe him, even though sincerity rang in his voice? She couldn't believe anything he said, anything he'd done. The room swam as she took in exactly what this meant. Their entire relationship was an orchestrated lie. She had been used. Worse, she had allowed him in, confided in him, opened up in a way she'd never opened up to anyone. Not even Izzy. Nausea swirled as she fought to show some control, hide a hurt so deep she couldn't begin to contemplate it. 'I'm leaving. Please don't contact me again.'

Damir didn't say anything, but then again why would he? He'd been well and truly caught out and there was nothing he could say or do to change that. He had no need to try and make her stay, any use he had for her was at an end. All Lily could do was gather the scattered remains of her dignity and leave. Head held so high her chin ached, Lily marched out of the study, retrieved her bag and shoes, stuffing the silver dress and wrap on top of her bikini. She didn't look back once as she headed for the door, resisting the urge to slam out of the villa.

The lush front garden stretched out before her, the gates tightly closed. She forced herself to move forward, swallowing a half-hysterical sob as question after question tumbled through her mind. Was this what happened when she tried to be impulsive? To have fun? Was this what happened when she let down her guard? Had this all trying to be a new person, to live a different way been a terrible mistake? Should she have stayed home and stuck with what she knew, what she'd been working for her whole life? Wouldn't that have been a better tribute to Izzy, to achieve the dreams that they'd first made together?

She walked slowly to the gate, the sun hot on her bare skin, pain throbbing deep inside. Reaching the gate, she pushed it, but it was locked. 'Dammit,' she cursed, looking around to see if there was a release button. She couldn't go back inside, and it was too tall to climb over. She stood there, irresolute, when she heard a voice behind her.

'Lily!'

Damir stood stock-still in the study and stared at the treacherous plans. How could he have been so stupid as to leave them out? It was almost as if he had wanted to betray himself, to let Lily know who he really was before things went any further.

He laughed, short and bitter. Who was he kidding? How much further could they go? He was already in too deep whether he liked it or not. But wasn't this what he did? Break promises, let people down, betray them? His father, Kata, and now Lily. She was better off knowing who he was, better off without him. He hurt and he betrayed, it was in his DNA.

With a muttered curse he turned around, not wanting to look at the plans, and strode towards the study door. He was ruthless, yes, he had to be. But he wasn't an out and out bastard. Was he? Was that who he'd become somewhere between his father's heart attack and the day Kata had walked out?

A beep caught his attention as he reached the door and Damir looked back, at the pile of paperwork lying on the table, at his phone flashing with who knew how many unread and unheard messages. There was always far more to do than any man could fit into a day, even when his day started at dawn and lasted long into the evening. He took a step towards the phone, trying to drag his mind back to where it needed to be, to the many things waiting for his attention, but all he could see was the anger blazing in Lily's eyes, at the stricken look on her face. A look he was responsible for.

He cursed again and then reeled around, making for the door, not allowing himself to think about what he was doing. Stepping out, he saw Lily standing by the gate, her back to him, slumped as if she'd given up. Shame shot through him. He'd seen her unhappiness that first day and disregarded it. He should do the decent thing, let her out, apologise then walk away and leave her alone. He didn't deserve to be forgiven, didn't deserve any kind of absolution.

'Lily!'

She looked over and her gaze caught his. There was no running away now. Holding her gaze as calmly as he could, Damir crossed the short distance between them, stopping just beyond touching distance.

Lily was the first to look away. 'What do you want? Because unless it's the key code for the gate I'm not interested.'

'Lily, I…'

He took a deep breath. *Never apologise for who you are*, his father had told him many times. *Never apologise for your am-*

bition, what it takes to do what you need to do. Damir had never stopped to think about those words before, to wonder if perhaps there was another way.

'I'm sorry.'

'Sorry for lying to me? Sorry for seducing me? For listening to me as if you cared? For making me start to think I could fall in love with you? You're going to have to narrow it down, I'm afraid.'

Every word fell with skilled precision. He was guilty as charged. 'I'm sorry for misleading you. You're right. I guessed who you were that first day and thought that if we became friends, you might put a good word in for me with Marija. I thought that if I got close to you I might get to know what her plans were before anyone else. I deliberately befriended you, that day on the beach just after you'd arrived, I sent you the flowers as part of a campaign to get you onside. But, Lily...' He stopped, trying to find the words. He didn't have any, but he had to say something.

'Lily, the rest of it, the spark between us, I didn't plan for that. How could I have? I don't understand it myself. I barely know you in many ways and yet I couldn't get you out of my head. I can't apologise for sleeping with you, because what we just shared was the one thing for a long, long time that felt real.'

Where on earth had all that come from? Damir had had no idea that he felt that way. But every word had been true. The vulnerability was terrifying, more terrifying than any leap of faith in business, than anything he'd ever done before.

Lily stopped walking, whirling round to glare at him. 'How dare you? How dare you say that to me?'

He shrugged. 'Because it's true.'

She stared at him for what felt like an eternity. 'Why?'

Damir's heart hammered harder than ever. He couldn't turn, couldn't look at her. 'What do you mean?'

When she spoke she sounded calmer, although sorrow laced her words. 'You have so much. Far more than I ever realised. When we first met, you gave me the impression that you owned a couple of businesses here in Lokvar, but actually you have quite the empire, don't you?'

'Yes.'

'And yet the villa is still so important you were prepared to do anything to get that as well?' She paused, but he didn't answer, the question clearly rhetorical. 'What happens next?'

'Lily, I—'

'You get your hands on the B&B, you tear it down, you replace half of that small but perfect coastline with another resort hotel, fill the beach with people who pay a fortune to stay there, change all that's special and unique about Fire Cove and then what? Will you be done? Or will you be onto the next project before the foundations are laid? Looking for the next person to charm and to help you on your way?'

Every word hit hard and accurately. His success had been as quick as it had been surprising in a country where connections still counted for everything, and talent and drive didn't always outweigh who you knew.

Throughout the last few years, Damir had managed to stay on the right side of the law, never venturing too far into the morally grey area, but he had had to be single-minded to do so. The price he'd paid, the price his ex-wife had paid, had been high. He told himself it was worth it. But Lily had struck to the heart of his doubt. When would it be enough? Would he ever feel that he had done enough or would he always keep striving to grow? To make more, be more?

'I don't know,' he said hoarsely. 'I just don't know.' But he did know. Whatever he achieved, it would never be enough.

'You told me once that you'd made a promise to your father. A promise to grow the business, to get the security he felt he'd never had. Is that what drives you? Is that how you justify what you do? If he were still here, would you still want to keep expanding so aggressively? Is that what he'd want?'

'It's all he ever wanted.'

'And would he think that the end always justifies the means? That what happened between us was okay?'

His laugh was bitter. 'Who do you think taught me, Lily? I am my father's son.'

Pain flashed in her eyes and Damir knew there was no coming back from this.

He had no case to plead. He let everyone down, that was who he was. He might be falling in love with Lily—hell, there was no might about it—but she was worthy of far more than him. The best thing he could do, the only thing he could do was to let her go and ensure she didn't waste a single moment thinking about him.

Somehow he managed a twisted smile. 'Lily, I like you. I like you a lot, more than I should. But I never pretended this was, that this could be anything more than a summer fling. I don't have the time or the emotional freedom for a relationship. What we share physically is amazing, I think it's a shame to waste that kind of chemistry. But let's not pretend this is something it isn't. Like I said, I'm sorry I misled you, but this isn't some big betrayal. We're just two people with a spark. Sex is sex, business is business. Don't confuse the two. But there's no reason we can't keep having fun.'

Lily had her answer, now it was time for her to walk away. She'd already been hurt, humiliated, but she was strong, no lasting damage had been done. Damir was ruthless, wasting more time on him would truly make her the fool she'd thought she was.

Until his last comment she'd hoped that he was the man she'd thought he was, the kind and compassionate man she glimpsed beyond the flirtatious façade. But she was wrong.

'Fun,' she repeated tonelessly. 'I see.' She did manage a smile then, but there was no warmth, no humour in it.

'Do you want to know what's ironic, Damir? Six months ago you would have been my ideal man. You're handsome and charming and a good lover, and you're driven. You wouldn't have expected anything from me and I would have been free to work as much as I wanted, to care as little as I needed. Maybe we would have gone on not expecting or caring, sleepwalked into a convenient marriage. But I'm not that woman any more. And you're no longer who I think I need or want. Maybe that's why it feels like you are. Maybe that's why somehow despite everything you have got under my skin, into my heart…' She stopped, swallowing back tears she was damned she'd shed in front of him.

'Don't worry, Damir. I'll put your case forward to Marija alongside my own. I'll be fair. But it's probably for the best we don't see each other any more. The fun is over.'

'If that's what you want.'

'I do.'

'Then goodbye, Lily. I'll open the gate.' And he turned and walked away. She watched him enter the house. He didn't look back once and so, as the gates slowly swung open and she left the villa, neither did she.

CHAPTER ELEVEN

DAMIR LOOKED AT his laptop, at the pile of documents waiting for him to read, to sign, to take action on and sighed. Despite burying himself in work for the last ten days, he was still nowhere near on top of it all. He'd let things slide over the last few weeks, taking days and evenings off. It was good to be back where he needed to be. Committed and focussed.

He leaned back in his chair and stared out of the window at his front gates. He could still see Lily standing there, tall and dignified and righteously angry. He saw her every time he looked at the gates, every time he entered his bedroom, or made a coffee, around every corner. He'd thought that the pain might have started to dim by now. It was only getting worse.

He missed her. Missed her laugh and her

smile. Missed the way she got to the heart of the matter, the way she made him think, the way she made him feel. Her warmth and her wit. Her touch. The feel of her under his hands.

He'd been asleep for so long and she had woken him. Was he really willing to drift back into that half-life again?

He jumped to his feet, prowling restlessly around the study, resisting the urge to text her, to call her, to hear her voice. Work had always, always helped in the past. Why wasn't it working now? No matter what he did, how many hours he put in, how many miles he travelled, he missed her. And now here he was, back where it had all started to unravel, and the pain of his loss was greater than ever.

Knowing that he had deliberately pushed her away was no help.

Walking over to the bookshelves, he pulled out a thin bound album and opened it. He hadn't looked at it for years. There he was. Much younger, much more naïve, much more hopeful, beaming in a suit, Kata beside him, his parents flanking them. They'd been only in their very early twenties when they'd married, still babies. Childhood sweethearts playing at being grown-ups. Would their marriage have survived if Damir hadn't checked out? Because although Kata had been the one to walk away, he had mentally left her long before, blaming her demands and his acquiescence for his father's death.

But there had been nothing wrong with her desire to spend time with her husband and he had been allowed to put his wife first. He could hear Lily telling him, 'It's very sad but no one's fault. Especially not yours.' She was right. He had to forgive himself and move on.

He flicked through the album, and to his surprise he felt no sorrow, no regret. Their marriage had been brief, but they'd been happy for a time. The truth was that theirs had been a young love, a first love, sweet and innocent but not robust enough to stand any great tests. The only fault lay in the way he had handled the unravelling of their relationship, the way he had distanced himself from Kata, the way he had locked his heart away since.

The way he'd treated Lily.

That was all on him.

He put the book away.

The way he felt about Lily was still so new, but different from anything he had ever felt before. Deeper, stronger, wiser. He was no idealist, not any more, but she had filled him with a hope he barely recognised, the possibility of a different kind of future, not sterile and lonely but filled with laughter and love. She made him want to do better, be better, be more. He didn't deserve her forgiveness and even if she bestowed it on him he had to accept that she would be unlikely to trust him again.

But how could he not try? He'd never expected, never wanted, to feel again, but she had broken down his barriers and reached his heart. It was time to put that heart on the line.

But, first, to really move on he had to face his past, and put it behind him once and for all.

Damir guided his car smoothly around the hairpin bends. On one side houses blended into the rocky countryside, on the other the sea sparkled far below in the afternoon

sun. Signposts pointed to the various resorts that served the hundreds and thousands of tourists who came to this part of
the Dalmatian Riviera.

A different kind of resort could also be
found along the coastline, a string of aban-
doned hotels, elite resorts from the commu-
nist era. His grandfather had once been a
chef in one of these hotels, but after the war
they had been left to crumble back into the
cliffs and beaches, ghost buildings incon-
gruous amongst the tourist-filled villages
and towns. As youths they had sailed there,
to party in the ruins, a rite of passage.

A sign directing traffic to the airport
flashed by and then at last he saw the
turning that led to Cavtat and he began
the drive down to the pretty harbourside
village. He found a parking spot at the top
of town, locked the car and set off, checking his phone for directions. The house he
sought was a pretty villa on the other side
of town. Painted a fresh pink with white
trim and glorious views, it felt prosperous
and loved. The garden was neat and well
tended and Damir noted children's toys
lined up on the porch, a swing set in the

garden. He swallowed, this was not going to be an easy visit.

He stood by the door for a moment, trying to summon up the courage, the resolve to knock but before he could do so the door opened. A petite, heavily pregnant woman, whose features he'd once known by heart, stared at him, arms crossed defensively. 'What are you doing here?'

'Hello, Kata.'

She glared for a moment longer before sighing. 'You'd better come in. I'm too big to stand at the door figuring out what you want.'

Ten minutes later he was sitting at her kitchen table, a coffee in front of him. The hallway and kitchen were as bright and cheery as the outside, this was clearly a well looked-after and happy family home. Looking around, he saw more signs of domesticity, a notice-board filled with appointments, letters and reminders, pinned-up children's drawings, and an open book lay face down on the table. A cat slunk around his ankles, purring loudly. Kata had always wanted a cat. He reached down to stroke the soft head and looked across at his ex-wife.

'When are you due?'

'Another six weeks.' She pulled a frustrated face. 'It's been much harder this time, being pregnant with a toddler and at the height of summer. Still, I shouldn't complain, it's what I always wanted.'

'You're happy then?'

She sank into the chair opposite him and stared searchingly into his face. 'Is that why you're here? Some kind of workaholic's twelve-step programme? You need absolution from everybody you hurt? Not that you deserve it, not from me.'

'I know.'

'But as you're asking, yes, I am happy. I'm married to a good man, a man who actually wants to be with me, who enjoys my company, who is satisfied with the life we lead. A man I love. I have a gorgeous, healthy son and a second child on the way. I've learned to appreciate every one of my blessings, and I am blessed.'

'I'm glad.' He meant every word of it. 'You deserve it.'

Kata huffed, but after a while her face

softened. 'Yes,' she said. 'I do. It took me a while to stop being so very angry with you, to be able to trust again, but I got there.'

'I am sorry,' he said softly. 'I'm not here for absolution, and probably don't deserve it, but I am sorry.'

'No, you don't. But it doesn't matter any more, Damir. I moved on a long time ago, as you can see. When I think about then, I don't feel angry or sad. I just feel sorry for the young, naïve people we were. I'm lucky I got to have a second chance, but I don't take my happiness for granted, I know it needs work and sacrifice and compromise on both sides.'

Kata drummed her fingers on the table, a gesture he remembered her making when she was unsure what her next step would be. 'How's your mother? She remarried, didn't she?'

'Yes, several years ago.' He grimaced. 'She's exactly the same, only more so. I don't see much of her, which is as much her choice as mine, more so maybe, but she seems happy. Her new husband is a politician, she finally gets to sit on the fundraising boards and attend the kind of events she always wanted to.'

He took a deep breath. 'I was wrong to allow her words to poison our marriage, Kata. I know now that I didn't cause my father's death, his heart did. He'd been warned to take it easy and he chose not to. That was on him. It's a tragedy, one I live with every day. But it wasn't my fault—and it absolutely wasn't yours, and I am so sorry I ever put that on you. You had every right to want to spend time with me, I had every right to keep weekends free to be with you. We weren't being selfish. But putting all the blame on us, on you, freezing you out, pushing you away, that was selfish. That was wrong. I didn't mean to hurt you.'

'I know. But you still did.' She leaned back in her chair, hands on her belly. It was strange to see her like this. Pregnancy aside she hadn't changed, barely looking any older than the twenty-four she'd been the last time he'd seen her. 'Why now? It's all over and done with, ancient history. I appreciate you making the effort to apologise, but why?'

'You've moved on. And I thought I had too. But while you've been creating a family, what have I achieved? The business is a lot bigger, sure. But I spend my evenings working alone. Money isn't the only way of measuring wealth, I know that now. And when it comes to love, you are richer by far. I met someone, and in doing so I've had to confront a lot of things about myself I don't like. How I behaved towards you is at the top of that list. An apology isn't enough, I know that. But it's heartfelt.'

She didn't answer for a long time. 'You've met someone. So, what, you've come to ask for my blessing?'

'No. I don't need or expect that. And it may be too late. I've hurt her too.' His short laugh was bitter. 'It's a pattern, isn't it? This time I'm going to learn from the past, I am going to try and fix things. But I couldn't do that without some closure from before, without telling you how much I wish I could have been a better husband, a better friend, been more honest with you, especially at the end.'

'In that case all I can say is good luck, Damir,' Kata said softly. 'Second chances don't come around all that often, don't mess this one up.'

'Thank you, Kata.' He pushed back his chair and got to his feet. 'For everything.'

'Goodbye, Damir.'

He stood for a moment, looking at the woman he no longer knew, content, happy, with a life in which he was just a footnote. And that was how it should be. He had many more chapters ahead of him, it was time to make sure they counted.

As always, the view was breath-taking, but Lily barely took it in, her eyes unfocussed and thoughts jumbled as she sat on the villa's porch, a coffee in her hand.

She had to stop wallowing, move on. It would be so easy to revert to her old self, go back to her office and her flat, her long days at her desk, her ambition and solitude, to tell herself that she'd tried and failed. Much harder to try and understand that being impulsive, being open to new experiences and new people was bound to lead her down the wrong path sometimes. After all, that was the very reason she'd avoided doing it her whole life.

One day she might look back and recognise that it was just bad luck that her first adventure had ended so badly. Damir had obviously recognised her emotional naïveté, her vulnerability. His decision to exploit that was on him, not on her.

But that reckoning was a long way off. First she had to get through the next few weeks, days, hours and minutes. Damir had hurt her. She'd liked him, or at least she'd liked the person she had thought he was, and she'd thought that he liked her too. More than liked. She had known she was falling for him, and had hoped that maybe he felt the same way. Thought he'd seen something in her that nobody else ever had, nobody apart from her family and Izzy.

'Oh, Izzy,' she whispered. 'You wouldn't have made such a stupid mistake, you were always better at reading people than me. What am I going to do? I finally fell in love, and it all went to pieces.'

In love. Not with the charming wooer or the tycoon but with the man she'd thought he was inside. A man with vulnerabilities and hurts, a thoughtful, funny man who made her body sing and her heart hope.

Even now, she couldn't help but think that that man existed, if only Damir could trust himself to care, to let people in.

But the fact remained that he had played her. He'd only ever approached her because of who she was, what she could do for him. She had opened up, shown all her vulnerabilities and fears to a man who had always planned to betray her.

She put her cup down decisively. Enough. Tomorrow was Izzy's birthday and she had promised her friend that she would celebrate. The B&B was only half-full, thanks to the wedding party cancellation, but the café-bar was as busy as ever. There was plenty for her to do to keep her mind off Damir. So she should get up and do it.

'Lily?' Ana was calling and slowly Lily got to her feet. 'Could you get the reception desk? We have some walk-ins asking if we have a room.'

'On my way,' she called back, straightening her shoulders and preparing her best hostess smile. Guests, work, keeping busy. That was the only cure for a broken heart, she knew. She just had to hope it worked.

She entered the villa through the side

door, dodging through the hot, busy kitchen, emerging into the bright wide hallway. Three people were waiting by the reception desk and as they turned recognition shot through her, followed by a relief so deep it almost floored her. 'Mum? Josip? Marija? What are you doing here?'

'We didn't want you to spend Izzy's birthday alone and when we realised the cancellation meant you had room for unexpected guests, we decided to come and join you,' her mother said.

'I'll always have room for you,' Lily stepped into her mother's arms and allowed herself to be held for several long minutes before hugging Josip, realising that he had come home after all these years for her. Gratitude filled her as she kissed his cheek.

'Marija's room has been kept clean and ready just in case she decided to come and check on us, and lucky for you two the best room is still available thanks to our flaky bride. I'll get Luka to take your bags up. Are you hungry? Of course you are. Let's find us all something to eat. I am so grateful you are here.'

* * *

They spent the rest of the afternoon catching up and showing Lily's mother around Lokvar, planning a few days of sightseeing for her—and for Josip who had left a very different place all those years ago. The next day, Izzy's birthday, they visited the Old Town. Memories of Damir were around every corner, but Lily resolutely pushed them away, determined to make new memories with her family, not dwell on old painful ones. During the day she tentatively raised her ideas for a foundation in Izzy's memory, grateful for her family's advice and input.

That evening Lily had planned a private dinner, tasking Antun to make a welcome-home feast of Dalmatian classics and setting up a table on the side terrace, away from the crowded and noisy bar. She was the first to change and come back downstairs and, grateful for a moment's reflective solitude, Lily wandered over to the swing seat and rocked gently, trying to absorb all that had happened in the last twenty-four hours, the last few weeks.

'Lily, are you all right?'

She looked up at the sound of Josip's voice and smiled, immediately moving up to make space for him, leaning against his reliable solidness. 'Of course. I am thrilled you are here. Thank you.'

'You needed me,' he said simply. And that right here was Josip distilled, what she and her mother needed, he provided. Somehow, Lily had never really appreciated that for over half her life she'd actually had the stability she craved. Josip had her back, always.

And this weekend he had proved his love by coming back to the country he had fled from all those years ago for her. She squeezed his arm. 'Has it been very hard? It can't be easy, seeing all your old haunts.'

'Haunts is the right word, there are ghosts everywhere.' He sighed, rubbing the dark stubble on his square, capable chin. 'But it has been good for me to come back and face them. I let it go on too long. It's not easy, walking around and listening to people talk about the city as a TV set, discussing fictional violence when last time I was here war was all too real, but the city has healed and moved on. I should too.'

'Easier said than done.'

'Always.' He paused. 'You know I don't like to pry, Lily, your secrets are yours, but is Damir Kozina the reason you've been so quiet, the reason for those shadows under your eyes?'

'There are no secrets on Lokvar,' she said, attempting to make light of the question.

'No secrets between my mother and Ana.'

'I suppose not. We were together and now we're not. These things happen.'

They rocked in silence for a moment before Josip spoke again. 'What's he like, Damir? Last time I saw him he was little more than a baby with determined eyes and a very stubborn will.'

Lily stared out to sea, searching for the right words. 'He's unsettled,' she said at last. 'He thinks the next project, the next deal will make him happy. Of course it won't, but he's too afraid to work out what will. Too afraid of his own feelings to try or to trust.' She smiled then. 'I see it because I was similar once, not that long ago.'

'His dad was the same. But *his* father,

Damir's grandfather, drove him hard. He was a difficult, bitter man, always wanted more, to be the best, to be in charge. He coveted this place, made several offers after the war, but it's been in our family for generations. My family would never consider it. In time Damir's papa became the same, obsessed with money and status, forgetting about the things that really matter.'

'When did you stop being friends?' Lily couldn't stop her curious questions, thirsty to know more about the man who somehow had crept into her heart.

Josip rocked the swing a few times before answering. 'We drifted apart rather than any one definitive moment. I wasn't here, of course, that didn't help, no internet or instant messages or texts in those days. And we didn't understand each other. After all, everything that made me want to leave Croatia made him want to stay. I tried to outrun my ghosts, he tried to build over his.'

'Damir may make his father and grandfather's dreams come true yet. You don't want the villa and although I considered buying it, even with Izzy's legacy I wouldn't have enough, and Damir will out-bid anyone else. I hope it makes him happy, although I hate the thought of seeing this place pulled down for one of his resorts. I'll have to look for somewhere else to base the foundation if that happens.'

'Would you buy it, if you could? Would you stay?'

'I would.' The words surprised her as she spoke them and she turned to Josip, eyes wide. 'I would! I'd have to diversify to make the villa pay through the off season, and I'd have to learn Croatian and to sail, and to cook a little for emergencies, and to learn to mix more than a gin and tonic, but I would. The last few months I've met such interesting people, it's a lot more fun than legal sub-clauses!

'And most importantly there's the set-ting. Waking up to this view, walking on the beach has brought me the kind of peace I didn't think existed. I'd love to stay. But it's a dream. I know that. Marija needs to fund her retirement and this is prime real estate, she needs to maximise what she can make from it. I just hope she puts clauses in to limit development. I don't know Croatian planning law but I would try and help if she wanted.'

'What she wants is for the villa to stay in the family, and you *are* her family. You're my daughter, Lily, you have been since the day I collected you from your grandparents to come and live with me and your mother, and I couldn't be prouder of you. I hope you know that. If you want to stay then the villa is yours, we both agreed that it should be. It wouldn't surprise me if this wasn't her plan all along.'

Lily stilled, trying to process his words. 'And you wouldn't mind?'

'Me? Not at all. Although I would have one condition, that you have a room for your mother and me when we need it. Now I've finally come back, I know I can't stay away so long. London is my home now, but Lokvar is part of me.'

'Always,' she promised. 'Always.'

'And Damir?'

Lily looked down at her hands. 'I don't know,' she said honestly. 'I don't know if I can ever trust him. He lied to me, and that's not something I can easily dismiss. It takes a lot for me to trust, and knowing

I got him wrong, that's hard for me. But he has his own problems, I don't think I'll be seeing him again. That's okay. I've survived much worse.'

'You were always stronger than you gave yourself credit for. And if Damir doesn't see that then he doesn't deserve you. I just want you to be happy, Lily.'

'I am,' she told him. 'At least, I have the tools to be. I will always miss Izzy, always, and I can't deny that I've been bruised by what happened with Damir, but at least I know I'm capable of wanting a relationship. He gave me that at least.'

Josip smiled and dropped a kiss on top of her head before heading back inside to find her mother. Lily held her smile until he'd gone and then let it slide off her face. She hadn't lied, she was ready to embrace her new life, the opportunities she had been given, the opportunities she wanted to create. But getting over Damir was going to take time. She just had to be patient and hope it didn't hurt for too long.

CHAPTER TWELVE

LILY GOT TO her feet and raised her glass, smiling at her family, her heart filled with love for these people who had travelled over a thousand miles to spend this day with her. Some things in her new life might have gone horribly wrong, but she still had so much to be thankful for.

'I'm not going to make a long speech you'll be glad to hear,' she said. 'But I do want to thank you with all my heart for coming and celebrating Izzy's birthday here with me today. I want to thank you for all the support you've offered in helping me find a way to remember and honour her. I especially want to thank Marija for giving me a chance to start anew and Ana for being so patient while I learned the ropes.' She paused, gathering her thoughts, catching first Josip's, then Marija's eyes, both full of confidence and belief. Belief in her.

'As you know, Lokvar, Fire Cove and this villa are very special places. I came here broken, and they healed me. And that gift is one I want to share with other people who need it, who need a break, to find out who they are and what they're capable of. I'm so happy that I will be able to see that happen.

'I had assumed that my stay would be short, one summer only, but I've been given the opportunity to try and make a home here and that feels more right than I could ever have imagined. Sorry, Ana, but we need to restart those Croatian lessons. Thank you all again, I hope you will visit me here often.' She looked up at the stars. 'Let's raise one final toast to Izzy.'

'To Izzy,' they chorused. Lily looked at each face in turn, her heart twisting with affection. Her mother, at peace after so many troubled years, was gazing at her with pride, Marija's smile was smug as if she had planned this very outcome—and maybe she had—while Josip looked more relaxed than he had in a long time.

There was still a lot to decide, a lot to organise, but she had a way forward. This move was nowhere in her life plans, but it felt right.

As she sank back into her seat, the whole table quietened and everyone stared at something—or someone—behind her. Lily felt his presence before she turned around, every nerve and sinew springing into life. She turned slowly to see Damir leaning against a tree, his hands in his pockets. He was formally dressed in one of his devastating suits, the tailored cut outlining the breadth of his shoulders and the length of his legs, but stubble shadowed his mouth and the hollows under his eyes mirrored hers.

'I'm sorry to interrupt,' he said. He sounded completely at ease, but his jaw was tight and his expression hooded. She swallowed, doing her best to seem as relaxed as him.

'That's okay,' she said. 'Mum, Josip, everyone, this is Damir. He owns the big hotel by the harbour.' She paused, not knowing what to say, what to do. Yell at him, cry, ignore him, throw him out? In the end good manners took over. 'Why don't you join us for a drink?'

She could sense her mother looking at him curiously, almost see Josip's protective hackles rising. Meanwhile Marija was leaning back in her chair, her bright eyes fixed on her neighbour speculatively.

Damir smiled. 'Thank you.' But he made no attempt to join them. 'Actually, there's something I need to say first.'

Lily couldn't read him, he was so rigid, his jaw set and eyes determined. 'Marija, last year I offered you twice what the villa was worth and you turned me down. I'd like to renew that offer today. Here in front of witnesses.'

The disappointment that flooded over Lily almost drowned her. He wasn't here for her, of course he wasn't. He was here for the villa. He knew her thoughts and dreams and yet he had marched in to hijack her remembrance dinner. Her hopes that there was a better man inside the ruthless tycoon were just that. Hopes. She could almost physically feel her heart break, an actual crack so loud she couldn't believe the whole table hadn't reacted. Nothing mattered to him but a deathbed promise and ambition, and woe betide anyone or anything who got in the way.

Her hands clenched on her glass. She shouldn't see it as a personal betrayal, she had known who he was. But like a fool she'd hoped that where she was concerned he could be better. She'd hoped she'd mattered. She'd hoped he'd fallen for her the way she'd fallen for him. But maybe he was incapable of that kind of feeling for anyone or anything that wasn't bricks and mortar.

'Damir...' She trailed off. She wanted to tell him that he was too late, that the villa was being given to her, that some things were more important than money. But it wasn't her place to say it. He was offering Marija a small fortune. Lily had to let her grandmother decide for herself.

'I want to buy the villa,' he repeated. 'For Lily. So that she can help children like her friend, so that she can make a difference.'

Hang on a minute. What had he just said? She was on her feet without realising it. 'You want to do *what*?'

Her family were almost unnaturally silent, as if their volume button had been turned off, looking from her to Damir, like spectators at a tennis match.

Damir took a step closer. 'I want to give the villa to you. I want you to live your dreams, Lily, whatever they may be. I want to help you live your dreams if you'll let me. I'm sorry I'm so late, I know this day is hard for you. But this is my gift to you. In memory of your friend. If you'll take it.'

The whole scenario felt unreal, like she was on stage only she had no idea of her lines or what happened next.

'I...' She had to get them away from their audience. 'Come with me.'

Lily jumped to her feet and marched away from the table and away from Damir towards the gate leading to the beach. She knew he was following her, that he would have followed her even without her instruction.

She didn't speak until they were out of earshot and then she turned. 'What's going on?'

This was it. This was his chance. He'd never felt so nervous in all his life. As if as all his happiness hinged on the next five minutes. And it did.

Damir took a deep breath and looked at Lily. She looked utterly beautiful in a flowery maxi dress, her hair caught up in a loose knot, tendrils caressing her cheeks. His chest ached with all he hadn't said, all he'd repressed. 'I love you.' It wasn't the speech he had prepared, but it was everything, it was all he that he had. Lily took half a step backwards, clasping her hands in front of her.

'I don't understand, where is this coming from?'

'I love you, Lily.' Now he'd finally said it, Damir was more emboldened, the words flowing naturally. 'I know we haven't known each other very long, but I love you. I think I have from the very first. From when I saw you here shouting defiantly at the sea.'

'From when you saw me and tried to figure out a way to use me,' she said, and he nodded.

'I did. And I am sorrier for that than I can say. But underneath the plans and the calculations and deceptions, there was something more, something driving me towards you, and that was terrifying. When you've spent as long as I have trying not to feel, you'll do anything to keep things that way, including lying to yourself.'

'Last time I saw you, you said we were just having fun.'

He grimaced. 'By then I had stopped lying to myself but I lied to you instead. I wanted you to walk away, you deserved so much more than I could give you. I thought that was the right thing to do.'

'And now?' She sounded cool, distant, but her fingers betrayed her emotion, twisting together, her eyes were bright with tears. Damir couldn't hold himself back any longer, couldn't restrain himself from offering her comfort, and he closed the short distance between them to take her hands, tilting her chin so he could look into her face, try and read her thoughts.

'I went to see Kata today. She has a son, another baby on the way, she's living the life she always wanted. And as I stood there, in her house full of toys and love and happiness, I realised that I am richer than even my father dared to dream, but I have nothing. Not if I'm too afraid to let anyone in. But I'm not afraid, not any more. And that's down to you.'

'Me?' Her voice trembled as she spoke the single syllable.

'After Kata left I decided that emotions just mess things up. That I was better concentrating on work, concentrating on things I could control. Then I met you and for the first time in a long time I felt something other than ambition. I lost control. And it terrified me. Feelings I didn't know how to manage threatened to break through and ruin all that hard-won peace.'

He paused, trying to find the words to show her, convince her of his sincerity. 'I recognised something in you from the first. I saw a woman who had experienced real tragedy and used it to move on. That shamed me, Lily. I allowed my past to define me, to hold me back, while you used yours to propel you forward.

'You have been through so much, more than I could ever imagine. Your childhood, the loss of your friend. It could have hardened you, turned you into someone like me, but instead you decided to embrace life, to get as much from it as you could. You make me want to be different, Lily, you make me want to be more. And that terrified me, because if I take away work then what's left? Who am I? Not Damir Kozina, hotelier, developer, investor but just Damir? I didn't know, and I wasn't brave enough to find out.'

'I don't know what to say, what to think,' she said, her fingers tightening around his, looking up at him with a mingled expression of hope and fear. 'You pushed me away so completely. I didn't expect to see you again, not properly. And now you're here and saying all this, trying to buy the villa for me. What about your dreams, your ambitions?'

'I still have them, but they have changed. I don't need to be bound by other people's visions, I need to find my own. I am sorrier than I can say for deceiving you. Although I'm not sorry for getting to know you, the times we spent together were the most special times of my life.'

He ran a finger down her cheek and felt her quiver under the light touch, she felt like coming home. 'You are clever and in-

sightful, you're funny and you're kind and
obviously you are insanely gorgeous. Those
are the reasons I'm attracted to you, but
you're more than that, you're made of steel,
you're resilient and strong and you care and
that's why I love you.'

That was it. That was all he had. His
heart on the line.

Lily stared up at Damir, barely able to process all he had said, let alone believe it.
'But how, why?' she said in the end, inar-
ticulately.

'We were watching the concert,' he said.
'And you'd just told me that you needed
my advice. That shook me. I'd been fool-
ing myself that we were just like any other
affair, that all we had was attraction. But
it wasn't true. You wanted more than my
money and my body, you wanted my opinion—I can't tell you how that felt. You
saw me, saw behind the mask. Maybe I
fell in love with you before that, when you
brought cakes on our daytrip to Dubrovnik.
You never just took, you always gave.'

'They weren't even very good cakes,' she
said, half in shock, and he laughed.

'They were amazing, because they were made with care and generosity. I realised at the concert that I didn't want to let you go, that the man I was when I was with you was a better, a happier man. But the last time I felt like that everything fell apart, my father died, my mother blamed me, my marriage disintegrated. I was terrified of what would happen if I acknowledged my feelings, acted on them. I was already distracted, making mistakes, unfocussed. It felt like history was repeating itself.

'When you discovered the plans, walked away, it felt almost fortuitous, gave me the opportunity I needed to step back, push you away. But that didn't help. And I couldn't help but ask myself who I was doing all this for. I told myself owning the villa, building a resort here would make me happy, but they were hollow lies. Nothing would make me happy if I was too scared to love, to really live.'

'You don't need to woo me with grand gestures, Damir. Buying the villa? It's too much.'

'Is it a grand gesture if I mean it? Your

vision is inspired, Lily. I just want to help you achieve it, in any way I can.'

Lily bit her lip. 'Marija has offered to give it to me, if I want to stay and run it. She's got quite a bit put by, so she's thinking of building herself a small home in the garden for when she's here and spending more time with Josip and mum the rest of the time.'

'So my grand gesture was unnecessary?' His smile was rueful and her heart melted.

'No. It was the single most thoughtful thing anyone has ever done for me.'

'I wanted to make a public declaration, I wanted you to know that I meant every word, that I was willing to make a fool of myself for you. Willing to do whatever it takes.' He stopped then and stared at her, eyes full of hope and love. Love for her. Lily's heart thumped almost painfully at the intensity in his dark gaze. 'Wait, Marija has given you the villa. Does that mean you're staying?'

'It does. Does that change things?' Her pulse speeded to rushing point as she waited for him to reply. It was one thing to open up to someone who was leaving, who would always be a romantic fantasy, quite another to do it to someone real, who would be there no matter what happened.

'Change things? I hope so.' He smiled properly then, sweet and sexy and so devastating her insides melted. 'I hope it means I get a chance to put things right, a chance to go back to the beginning and woo you the way you should always have been wooed. To see where this leads when time is on our side, to hope it leads to a home like Kata's, one filled with love and happiness. Is that possible, Lily? Would you be able to give me a second chance?'

Lily didn't answer for a long moment, trying to make sense of her jumbled thoughts. Damir had hurt her and understanding why didn't change that. But understanding him made it easier. 'I didn't come here looking for anything but a way to heal. Meeting you, meeting anyone, wasn't part of the plan.' She reached up and cupped his cheek. 'From the start I suspected you were too good to be true—and then I found out how you planned to use me. Fool me once...' Her voice trailed off.

'I know I made mistakes. Asking you to trust me again is a lot.'

'It is.'

Lily hesitated. The sensible thing would be to say thanks but no thanks. To walk away with her dignity intact if not her heart. But the hope and sincerity blazing out of Damir's face, in his voice, his whole body made her pause and hope, more than his grand gesture to buy the villa.

Go on, she could hear Izzy urge her. *Give him the chance to prove himself to you. Don't be afraid, Lily.*

'It is a lot,' she replied. 'But so is taking on permanent management of a B&B and trying to run it all year round. I suppose it would be useful to have an expert on hand to help me figure it out. And I've heard it can get cold and lonely on Lokvar in the winter months. A local man might be just what I need.'

It took him several incredulous seconds to respond but then Lily found herself swept up and whirled around. 'You won't regret it,' Damir vowed.

'I know,' she said, smiling up at him. 'Because I love you too and I don't give my heart away easily or often, Damir. So I have to trust you to be careful with it.'

'I will. Always.' And then he finally kissed her, a kiss filled with all the pent-up love and emotion, an almost overwhelming kiss that consumed her entire body. 'Always,' he murmured against her mouth. 'I love you, Lily, and I will spend every day proving it to you, if it takes the rest of my life.'

'I love you too.' And as she kissed him back, Lily knew her heart was safe with this man, in this place, and that hard as the past had been, with Damir by her side her future would be more than she had ever dared dream possible.

EPILOGUE

One year later

LILY WALKED OUT of the villa, cake in her hands, and paused, taking in the scene below. It was almost as if she had stepped in a time machine and she was back to this point one year ago. The table was set on the private terrace, her mother, Josip, Marija and Ana were sitting around it, the remains of a delicious meal still on their plates.

But this year there were extra guests. Damir was sprawled on one side of the table, gently flirting with Marija and Lily's mother, and Janet, Izzy's foster mother, had come over to celebrate Izzy's birthday, bringing the two teenagers she currently fostered, the first beneficiaries of the Isabella Burton Foundation. They were here for two weeks of rest and relaxation for Janet and activities and sunshine for the kids.

'I hope you'd be happy, Izzy,' she said softly. 'They're having a great time, and Tia is already asking about coming over to work when she's eighteen. She reminds me of you. Lots of drive, lots of ambition and plenty of brains' She looked up at the stars for a long moment. 'I miss you. I'll always miss you.'

She blinked back tears, pasting on a smile as she carefully carried the cake down to the table. Antun had outdone himself and the lavishly decorated confection deserved all the oohs and aahs that greeted it, and her smile widened and became genuine as she set it carefully in front of Ana, who was the best cake cutter in the villa.

'You look happy, Lily,' Josip said as she took her seat next to him. 'Happy and well.'

'I am happy,' she told him. 'It was the right decision, to spend the off season in Dubrovnik in Damir's villa, and the summer here. I still think there are ways to make the villa productive through the winter but setting up the foundation, trying to learn Croatian and learning to sail were important too.'

'No regrets?' he asked her, and she smiled, her gaze settling on Damir, relaxed and at ease, and more handsome than ever, at least in her totally biased opinion.

'None at all. This felt like home the day I first woke up here and now I can't imagine living anywhere else. I'm just glad Marija decided to work one last season. I'm learning so much from her. I'm also so happy you and Mum have visited so often.'

'It's taken time but I've found my peace with the past,' Josip said. 'I'm glad you have as well, Lily. You deserve all the happiness.'

At that moment Ana passed her a slice of the chocolate orange cake and Josip's attention turned to comparing the size of his dessert to Tia's and Leo's, good-naturedly protesting that they had far bigger slices than he did. Lily leaned back and looked around the table, counting all her blessings as she did so. She lived in a place she loved with a man she appreciated more every day, doing a job she found rewarding whilst spending the long off season learning about the culture of the beautiful country in which she now lived. She didn't think she could possibly be happier.

The dinner finally came to an end, and as the teenagers began to help Ana clear the table, Damir slipped his arms around Lily's waist, kissing her neck as he did so, and she leaned gratefully back against him.

'I've missed you,' he said.

'Then you shouldn't take such long business trips,' she said, and felt his laughter rumble through her.

'I hurried home as soon as I could. Walk with me?'

'Of course.' It was their usual custom to walk along Fire Cove after dinner as long as Lily wasn't working. She often thought this moment, hand in hand with the sun setting around them, was her favourite part of the day.

'It's so beautiful here,' she said, as they walked past the last of the tourists onto the quieter part of the beach. 'I know I say it every day, but it's true every day.'

'It is.'

'Glad you didn't turn it into an exclusive resort?' And he smiled.

'I wouldn't go that far, but the area I've found is spectacular. I can't wait for you to see it when it's done.' But he sounded distracted.

Lily squeezed his hand. 'Are you okay?'

He started. 'Yes, fine.'

They carried on until they reached the end of the beach but they didn't stop there, Damir leading her over the rocks until they reached the tiny curve of sand, flanked by rocks and dunes and sea where they had first made love.

'I love it here,' she said softly, looking out at the boats bobbing up and down on the far horizon. 'It's like our own secret beach.'

'Yes.' He sounded distracted again and she turned to look at him. 'Damir?' She faltered to a stop. 'What are you doing?'

He was on one knee, a small velvet box in one hand. 'What does it look like I'm doing? No, ignore that, that wasn't in the script.'

'The script?'

'I wanted this to be perfect.' Damir was usually the most confident-seeming person she knew, but he didn't look confident now, his throat working as he seemed to search for words. 'I want this to be perfect, because you are perfect. Lily, I love you. You brought the sunshine into my life and the hope into my heart and have given me more happiness than I ever thought possible. I want nothing more than to keep loving you, laughing with you and to grow old with you. Would you, Lily Woodhouse, do me the very great honour of becoming my wife?'

He flipped open the box to reveal a beautiful ring, a sapphire flanked by diamonds, and Lily gasped.

'Oh, Damir. Yes, of course I will.'

He smiled then, boyish and so handsome it took her breath away. 'That is good, because there is champagne chilling behind that rock and I asked Josip and your mother's permission this morning...' He paused then. 'I hope you don't mind, I know you don't need anyone's permission to do anything...'

'No, I don't mind.' Her heart turned over with love and thankfulness for his thoughtfulness. 'Thank you for including Josip and showing him how important he is to me. Wait, they both said yes, didn't they?'

'After a very long time,' Damir admitted, getting to his feet and extracting the ring from the box. Lily held out her left hand, feeling unaccountably shy as Damir slid the ring onto her third finger.

'It's perfect,' she said, cupping his cheeks and rising up to kiss him.

'So are you,' he said, looking into her eyes. 'So are you.'

* * * * *

If you enjoyed this story,
check out these other great reads from
Jessica Gilmore

Bound by the Prince's Baby
Reawakened by His Christmas Kiss
Cinderella's Secret Royal Fling
Honeymooning with Her Brazilian Boss

All available now!